Billion-Dollar Bachelors

Business isn't the only thing making their heads spin!

Meet three billionaire friends—Ted Fincher, Sawyer Mahoney and Ronan Gerard—who channeled their brains, brawn and ambition to start the mega-successful Big Think Corp. Their aim is to save the world, one project at a time!

But while they have success in business, their love lives need work! When Ted is interviewed by effervescent journalist Adelaid, things turn passionate, and they have a shocking surprise in store.

Sawyer attends the birthday party of his best friend's sister, and when reunited with Petra, feelings they thought they had buried long ago come crashing to the surface...

Ronan is very protective of receptionist Hadley. But after she resigns, they begin to disentangle the ties that have bound them this far, to find that they've been entangled in a whole other way all along!

Find out what happens in Ted's story in
Whirlwind Fling to Baby Bombshell

And don't miss Sawyer and Petra's story
Fake Engagement with the Billionaire
Available now!

Look out for Ronan and Hadley's story
Cinderella Assistant to Boss's Bride
Coming in 2023 from Harlequin Romance!

Fake Engagement with the Billionaire

—

Ally Blake

Recycling programs
for this product may
not exist in your area.

ISBN-13: 978-1-335-73715-1

Fake Engagement with the Billionaire

Copyright © 2023 by Ally Blake

For questions and comments about the quality of this book, please contact us at CustomerService@Harlequin.com.

Harlequin Enterprises ULC
22 Adelaide St. West, 41st Floor
Toronto, Ontario M5H 4E3, Canada
www.Harlequin.com

Printed in U.S.A.

Australian author **Ally Blake** loves reading and strong coffee, porch swings and dappled sunshine, beautiful notebooks and soft, dark pencils. Her inquisitive, rambunctious, spectacular children are her exquisite delights. And she adores writing love stories so much she'd write them even if nobody else read them. No wonder, then, having sold over four million copies of her romance novels worldwide, Ally is living her bliss. Find out more about Ally's books at allyblake.com.

Books by Ally Blake

Harlequin Romance

Billion-Dollar Bachelors

Whirlwind Fling to Baby Bombshell

A Fairytale Summer!

Dream Vacation, Surprise Baby

The Royals of Vallemont

Rescuing the Royal Runaway Bride
Amber and the Rogue Prince

Hired by the Mysterious Millionaire
A Week with the Best Man
Crazy About Her Impossible Boss
Brooding Rebel to Baby Daddy
The Millionaire's Melbourne Proposal
The Wedding Favor

Visit the Author Profile page
at Harlequin.com for more titles.

To my rubber band friends—Cassandra, Rowena and Sangeeta. For your foundational friendship, the lockdown Zoom drinks and, of course, Binga. I'm so grateful that, despite time and distance, we keep tugging one another back. xxx

Praise for
Ally Blake

"I found *Hired by the Mysterious Millionaire* by Ally Blake to be a fascinating read... The story of how they get to their HEA is a page-turner. 'Love conquers all' and does so in a very entertaining way in this book."

—*Harlequin Junkie*

CHAPTER ONE

PETRA GILPIN HAD made a huge mistake.

Since she was knee-high to a butterfly Petra's intuition had been her navigation system, bewildering her highly successful Type A parents, and delighting her older brother Finn.

It had sent her meandering down garden paths in search of soft pink feathers and sparkly pink stones to add to her collections. It had sent her to art school, where she'd discovered her skills were more in the appreciation than the doing. And it was entirely to blame for her losing her heart to the first boy who'd found a pink feather on the ground one day and saved it for her.

Petra's instinct was not infallible by any means. It had got her lost more times than she could count. But only in the best ways.

Now, sitting in the swanky Gilded Cage nightclub, the deeply luxurious purple velvet couch making the backs of her knees itch, that same intuition buzzed at her like crazy.

Petra glanced at her bag—the tip of her flamingo phone case in particular.

Read it, her intuition whispered, referring to

the email that had lured her back home to Melbourne for the first time in over a decade. *Read it one more time. There's got to be a loophole, a way out—*

"This place is insane!" said Deena—one of the few friends from her weekly boarding school days she'd actually kept in touch with—climbing through the actual cage curving around their private booth, huge bottle of bubbly in hand. "Did you see the disco ball over the dance floor? It's bigger than my office. And I made partner last year. Having fun?"

Petra twinkled a smile her way. And wondered at what point she could call it a night.

Deena refilled their glasses generously, before lifting hers in the air. "What shall we toast to?"

Petra always raised a glass to the same thing—her big brother Finn. But Deena hadn't met him, which would be a little weird.

"You choose," Petra said.

"Your welcome home?"

Petra felt her nose twitch.

Deena laughed. "Okay, not that. How about beauty, love, art and…hot men with roping arm veins?"

Petra perked up and clinked glasses and said, "To favourite things!"

As the excellent bubbles dived deliciously down her throat, Petra pondered if *huge mistake* might be pushing it. For Deena was good value.

And the club's design elements were exquisitely brassy and bold. It was just that Petra was more a behind-the-scenes, get-it-done-then-head-home-for-a-glass-of-red kind of girl.

A burst of joyful noise saw Deena on her knees on the couch, leaning through the bars, making friends with the hen's night party in the private cage next door.

Petra took her chance, grabbing her phone.

DARLING!

That was how the email in question began. Because that was her mother's way of showing she felt fondness towards her daughter, even though she'd spent Petra's entire childhood acting as if Petra had simply wandered in from the garden one day, and Josephine had decided raising her as their own was the civilised thing to do.

And all in caps because her mother had read that it expressed urgency, and deemed every message she ever sent out into the world to be of great import.

Petra nibbled at her thumbnail as she read on.

YOU MIGHT REMEMBER THAT YOUR FATHER AND I ARE ON THE BOARD OF THE GALLERY OF MELBOURNE.

THE GOM HAS FOUND ITSELF IN A BIT OF A FIX AND IN NEED OF SOMEONE WITH

YOUR UNCOMMONLY SPECIFIC SKILL SET, AS WELL AS A NAME THAT WILL INSPIRE TRUST IN THOSE BEST ABLE TO DONATE THE FUNDS THAT IT NOW RATHER DESPERATELY REQUIRES IN ORDER TO KEEP ITS DOORS OPEN.

I MUST INSIST ON YOUR DISCRETION ON THIS POINT. AFTER SOME YEARS OF MISMANAGEMENT THE SITUATION IS DIRE. WE'VE THUS FAR HELD OFF THE WHIFF OF SCANDAL AND WISH FOR IT TO REMAIN THAT WAY.

YOUR FATHER AND I REMEMBER HOW MUCH YOU ENJOYED YOUR TIME SPENT IN THE GALLERY AS A CHILD, AND HOPE THIS MIGHT ENCOURAGE YOU TO DO WHAT MUST BE DONE.

ARE YOU UP FOR THE CHALLENGE?

Petra's response—lots of *wows* and exclamation marks and Some of the best memories of my childhood, followed by a final Challenge accepted! were all typed in a shocked flurry, as if it was the best news ever.

Yes, art was her field, but not the business side—more the enchantment that came with stumbling on a work that made a person *feel* something. An affinity that had led to her procuring private collections for princes and pop stars, curating modern art collections for famous galleries, and breaking records hosting auctions of digital art.

All of which she'd put on hold so that she might help her parents save the august, old Gallery of Melbourne.

The sounds of the club whumped back to her, and Petra lifted her glass to find it empty.

"Phone down!" said Deena, literally yanking it out of Petra's hand and tossing it up the other end of the couch. "No work. Or cat memes. Or whatever your kink is these days. And no photos. What happens at the Gilded Cage stays at the Gilded Cage."

Petra held out her glass and Deena happily refilled it. "What exactly do you imagine happening tonight?"

Deena reared back, hand to her throat. "I am happily married! It's my mission to see *you* hooked up."

Petra flinched. "You're meant to be giving me a rundown on who the movers and shakers are in Melbourne these days. Hooking up was not on the agenda." Or bubbly, for that matter, but there she was, glass in hand.

"It can be!" said Deena. "Unless you have a man back in London?"

Petra shook her head rather more vehemently than was probably necessary. It wasn't as if she didn't *date*, it was just another *normal person* thing that didn't come naturally to her.

She *had* thought herself on the way to falling in love a couple of years back, with a soft-spoken junior taxidermist at the American Museum of Natural History. It had taken her longer than it ought to realise that rather than being a strong silent type—her catnip—he was pathologically shy. And what she'd liked *most* about him was that he didn't make her feel as if she had to *work* to impress him.

Had she imagined she'd still feel the sting of her parents' lack of insight into who she was at thirty? Heck, no. Then again, she *had* imagined she'd be married to her favourite football player and living in some beautiful, gloriously eclectic hideaway in the Dandenong mountains by now.

"Humour me," Deena begged, then poked her head through the bars of their cage as she looked down on the dance floor. "Nope. Not him. Wait a minute… *Ding! Ding! Ding!* I do believe we've found a winner! And—holy mother of Thor—he might just be the most beautiful man who ever lived."

"Big call," said Petra, snuggling deeper into the couch as she sipped on her bubbly.

"Big's the word," said Deena. "This guy is huge. Rugged. Beastly. Smells like summer rain."

Petra laughed, the sound now bubbly too. She spun, fluffing her long dusky pink tulle skirt behind her so she could hop up onto her knees and see what the fuss was about. Only for the lights bouncing off the glassy mosaic ceiling to do funny things to her balance, making her wonder exactly how many times Deena had refilled her glass.

"How can you possibly tell what he smells like from here?" Petra asked.

"It's a skill. Hang on, I've lost him. How could I lose him? Dark curls, the build of a giant, brown leather jacket… There!" Deena called, finger pointing madly.

Petra followed the line of the finger. And before she could mouth the words, *Which one?* a voice inside her head said:

That one.

The seething Saturday night crowd seemed to pause and take a breath, clearing a path to where a hulking, dark-haired man leant his heft against the circular neon bar in the centre of the room. Even from that distance Petra could sense the slow roll of a meaty shoulder before the guy lifted a glass to his mouth, the dark hair curling wildly and overlong over the collar of his beaten-up brown leather jacket.

It was enough for Petra to plonk her backside back into the seat, the tulle crinkling as it settled around her.

It couldn't be *him*, could it?

He was *always* travelling, from country to country, city to city, even village to village, spreading Big Think Corp fairy dust—aka tech, or insight, or provisions—on whoever needed it. It had been years since they'd been in the same time zone, much less the same city.

And yet…

If her intuition had been humming before, now it filled her head with a delirious high-pitched scream.

"Hey," Deena cried, "why are you not down there, shoving people out of the way to get to him? I would if I wasn't, you know, happily married."

"Too brooding for my taste," Petra lied as she downed the remains of her bubbly in one mighty gulp. But, rather than loosening her up, it tightened her insides like the squeeze of a rubber band.

Deena settled her chin against her hand and sighed. "Yeah, you're probably right. All that testosterone must be a lot to handle. A guy who knows how to rock cycling gear, and brings you coffee in bed every morning, that's the ticket. That's *my* man and I'm…"

"Happily married." Petra shot Deena a smile.

Deena smiled back. "Now, I have to take a quick trip to the ladies' room. Then I might find someone to dance with me. Platonically. Wanna come with?"

Petra saw the bottom of yet another empty glass. "I might grab some water."

Deena patted her on the knee before climbing over her legs and out of the cage. "See you in a bit, then."

"Here goes," Petra said, ducking under the arch of their twirling gilt cocoon, strappy high heels carefully navigating the small steps down to the dance floor below. The music felt as if it was rising from the floor, through her knees and into her spine.

Once she reached the other side she ducked into a spare slot at the busy bar, then lifted onto her toes and glanced along the bar. Finding no familiar faces at all, she slumped back to her heels in disappointment.

Then stared dreamily at the pink lights dappling her skin, reflected off a thousand tiny mirrors embedded in the roof above, wishing she could bottle it somehow.

"What can I get you?"

Petra looked up to find a bartender smiling her way. The word *water* danced on her tongue before it was somehow replaced with, "Tequila. Slammer."

The bartender clocked her fob, their private booth coming with its own eye-watering bar tab.

The moment the bartender put the ingredients in front of her she dabbed salt on her wrist, licked it off with a quick determined swipe of her tongue and downed the clear spirit in one go.

Wincing as she bit down on the sliver of lemon, she reached up into her hair, fluffed the roots till her auburn waves settled around her face like a cage of their own. And she let the tequila do what the bubbly had not, sear her fluctuating intuition away.

"Good evening," a male voice said beside her, the cloying scent of cologne following.

"Nope," said Petra, not even turning.

"Let me buy you a—"

"Nope," she said again. Eyes now closed, she smiled as she felt the space beside her cool as the interloper moved away.

But it was short-lived, as soon a wall of heat filled the gap. A deeper male voice said, "Of all the gin joints in all the world."

Only this time the rusty tone made her skin prickle, her breath catch and her instincts rise within her like a hurricane.

Eyes fluttering open, Petra braced herself and turned. But there was no amount of bracing to combat the rush of heat swooping her insides as she came face to face with the man in the battered leather jacket.

"Sawyer," she said on a heady exhalation of breath.

Sawyer Mahoney. Her late brother Finn's best friend. The one who'd gifted her a pink feather all those years ago. The most beautiful man who had ever lived.

The last time she'd seen him in the flesh had been a year or so after Finn died. At her eighteenth birthday party. Where they'd made one of those romcom movie pacts, promising to marry if neither was hitched by her thirtieth birthday. Not that that was why she hadn't seen him since. She didn't think.

Sawyer looked just the same, only different, if

that made any sense. His lashes were still impossibly long, though creases now branched from the edges of his clear blue eyes, while sparks of grey glinted within the curls and the thick stubble covering his hard jaw.

It suited him. Boy, did it suit him.

As she stood there, cataloguing every part of him, his mouth cocked at the corner, his expression questioning.

And finally the very fact of him there, *right there*, overwhelmed her completely and Petra threw herself into his arms.

"Whoa," he said, his voice muffled by her hair.

Then, after the merest hesitation, his arms closed around her too. Strong arms, thick, like tree branches. Tightening. As if he too was more than merely glad to see her.

They'd kept in touch over the years. Long, zingy text chains, funny social media comments—his to her, as he never posted a thing—memes shared. Though it had taken Petra a couple of years to realise Sawyer was trying to fill the gap Finn had left somehow.

Not that he'd ever admitted as much.

Not that that was what she'd *ever* wanted from him.

This, she thought, *this was what coming home was meant to feel like.*

Like a pool of warm lamplight. Like curling your feet beneath you on the couch.

Which was why she held on tight, even when she found herself noticing the press of his thighs against hers. The dig of his jeans button at her hip. The scent of him filling her nostrils. No cologne. Just him. Earthy and warm and delicious.

When she began to imagine the grip of his fingers around her waist shifting, pulling her closer still, she knew it was time to let go. Her ability to see magic where others did not might be her greatest asset when it came to her work, but when it came to Sawyer Mahoney it had always been a one-sided affair.

After indulging in a final deep breath, Petra lifted her head out of the cocoon of his chest and pulled herself completely from the circle of his arms.

"It's so good to see you!" she said, thumping him on the chest with a fist, reminding herself that they were old chums.

Had been since she was fourteen, and he sixteen, and Finn had brought him home from footy practice looking like a Labrador puppy, all muddy limbs and knotted hair, and eyes so clear she'd had to blink to make sure he was real.

Only her fist bounced. He was harder than he used to be. Time had hewn him into solid rock. And if her knees gave way, just a little, she covered it well.

"What are you doing here?" She glanced pointedly at the huge mirror ball over the dance floor, the hot pink bar stools, the confetti painted into the bar.

Sawyer's half-smile kicked higher again. She imagined the deep, sensual bracket bracing the edge of his lips, now hidden beneath a beard, as he said, "Right back at ya, kid."

The bubbles in her blood went *pop-pop-pop*.

Kid. He hadn't called her that since she was, well, a kid. She'd always be Finn's little sister in his eyes, and it was better to remember that than, you know, lust.

"Oh, I'm fancy now," Petra said, hands out, rocking back and forth to show off her pink tulle dress. "Gave up the overalls and bare feet for grown-up clothes a while back now."

His gaze didn't shift, but she felt him take her in. And move closer as the crowd pressed in around them. The music seemed to lift a notch. Faster, deeper, vibrating in Petra's chest now, her belly. Lower.

Before she did something really silly, like sigh, or grab his sleeve and roll it up to see if he still had those amazing veins, Petra leapt in with, "Aren't you meant to be in Guatemala? Or Istanbul? Or Flub…istan…ovia?"

"Flubistanovia?"

She waved a hand. "I don't keep tabs."

She did, of course. It wasn't that hard.

Just after her eighteenth birthday party he'd run off to become an Australian Football League star—which had been his, and her brother's, dream. After a career-ending injury, he'd been in rehab for months and had used his spare time to fight for better rehab funding for vulnerable kids. Which had won him the Young Australian of the Year award.

To say he was beloved by the press—and therefore easy to cyber-stalk—would be an understatement.

And that was all before he'd co-created Big Think. A *multi-billion-dollar future-proof powerhouse focused on world health, innovation and invention, and Third World equity*. Yes, she'd memorised the mission statement on their website by heart.

No wonder he was one of the most written-about men in the country.

As if he could hear her thoughts, he turned a little to face the bar, keeping the crowd at his back. Petra gazed about but couldn't see anyone paying them any attention. Probably because he looked so scruffy, so rough.

"Are you in town long?" she asked, mirroring his pose.

"A bit. A few weeks at least. You?"

"Same," she said, bumping her arm against his, as if needing to make sure he was really there.

"What are the odds?" he said, his voice low.

Something flickered behind the blue, something warm, molten, too quick to catch. And the rubber band feeling was back, tugging her towards him. But, despite the tequila-induced warmth moving through her, she held her ground.

"You here on your own?" she asked.

His mouth quirked. "I was meant to be meeting Ronan."

"Ronan's *here*?" Petra had known Ronan Gerard, one of his Big Think co-owners, longer than she'd known Sawyer, and could picture him in a place like this even less than she could Sawyer.

Sawyer lifted his drink and downed the last sip. "Not, as it turns out. I believe he thought it a great joke to have me come here, straight from the airport, under the guise of an important meeting."

"Ah," said Petra, chuckling.

Like the Gilpins, the Gerards enjoyed the rarefied world of trust funds and private schooling and summers in Europe. Ronan had fought against it, in his own way, whereas Finn had leaned in, enjoying the trappings. Petra had simply *never* fitted in. Ever.

While Sawyer, having come from more humble beginnings, with far more responsibility loaded onto his shoulders from a young age, stood up, fought the good fight and did what had to be done.

"Finding new and interesting ways to amuse himself is a mental health necessity where Ronan's concerned."

Sawyer nodded. Then ran a hand up the back

of his neck. Was that dust he'd dislodged, now floating about his head?

She reached and brushed some from his shoulder. "How did they even let you on the plane, looking like this?"

"We have our own jet."

Of course. "Well, you're a grub. Wherever you've come from, you brought it with you."

Spying a few stray flecks, she swiped a finger down the bridge of his nose, her thumb grazing the line of his cheek. She felt him still. Her gaze flicked back to his in time to see a shadow pass over his eyes.

Swallowing, she let her hand drop. And when she caught the bartender's eye she motioned for another drink.

"You never mentioned you were coming home," Sawyer said.

Petra explained her mother's email, the job offer that came with it, her hope that Deena could help her make some local connections.

In fact... She looked at Sawyer. *He* was a connection. He and Ronan could fulfil her budget with their spare change. Then she could head off into the sunset, having proven to her parents that she was, in fact, pretty fabulous and worthy of their regard.

"You okay there?" Sawyer asked, his gaze dropping to her mouth.

No doubt because she was nibbling on her bottom lip as if it was made of chocolate. "Yep! Fine. Great."

His eyes narrowed, and she felt the shift in him. He stood taller, rolled his shoulders, made himself even bigger somehow. Protection mode engaged. "If you need my help—"

She held up a hand, close enough to his face his eyes crossed slightly. Close enough to feel his breath against her palm. She moved it back. A smidge. "I've got this."

When his eyes found hers they were glinting. "What if I want to help the art?"

Her resolve faltered under the warmth of his tone. "And how would you propose to do that?"

"Say, if the gift shop is selling a poster of a kitten with a funny saying written over it, you could put one aside for me."

"Not dogs playing poker?"

He thought about it then shrugged. "Nah. Kittens all the way."

"Fine," she joked. "That'll be a hundred grand."

"Mercenary." Sawyer flashed a grin.

Petra couldn't help but grin right on back.

For Sawyer was in town. For a bit. As was she.

Yes, her contract with the old Gallery of Melbourne might come with complications, but for the first time since she'd read her mother's email daring her, *ARE YOU UP FOR THE CHALLENGE?* Petra felt a thrill of anticipation rush through her.

"Here you go," the bartender said, placing her tequila on the bar. He gave Sawyer a second glance, as if trying to place him, before shaking his head.

"Want one?" she asked, lifting her drink. "Or are you going to make me drink alone?"

A muscle flickered under his eye. Then he nodded his acquiescence to the bartender.

A minute later a second tequila shot was lined up beside hers.

Petra flashed her fob. "On me," she explained to Sawyer.

"There's no need. I—"

"I'm paying. Told you I'm a fancy grown-up now."

Sawyer let that sink in before lifting his glass. "What should we drink to? Good health? Good weather?"

"To Finn," she said, closing her eyes and sending out a small happy thought to her brother, as she always did.

She opened her eyes in time to see myriad emotions flashing across Sawyer's eyes—shock, sorrow, and a flicker of something that looked a hell of a lot like guilt.

"Sorry," she said, not quite sure what she was apologising for. "We can toast something else?"

Sawyer pulled everything back inside himself, locked it down, breathed out and shook his head. "No, it's fine. It's a good choice."

It was, right? For Finn was there between them in every conversation they had. When it came down to it, everything they were, everything they were *not*, all came down to Finn.

"You *absolutely* sure?" she asked.

"Petra," he warned. Her name, in that voice, was enough to stop her arguing further.

"Okay then," she said. Then, with gusto enough for both of them, she added, "To Finn."

A muscle ticked in Sawyer's jaw before he nodded, downed the drink in one go and said, "Another?"

Petra knew water was probably a really good idea. But so was flossing, and she didn't do that nearly as much as she ought to. Doing what she was *supposed* to do had never been her thing. That was where her instincts came in. And in that moment they were feeling pretty buzzed.

"Bring it on," she said.

"May as well leave the bottle," Sawyer said, raising his glass to the bartender.

Petra shot Sawyer a look. "Like that, is it?"

"It's been a hard few months," he said.

"Hard?" she said, leaning her chin on her hand and batting her lashes his way.

"Long."

Petra grinned as the words floated between them in a bubble of double meanings, while Sawyer slowly shook his head, trying to hide his smile.

The bartender lined up their drinks, then accepted the sneaky hundred Sawyer passed across the bar.

"Ready?" Petra asked, watching him as she licked the knuckle of her thumb.

"Not even close," he said, shaking his head before licking his knuckle too.

Petra poured salt on the slicks of damp. Took the lemon slice he offered. Then tapped her glass against his.

"To Finn," he said, his voice like sandpaper, as if it was the first time he'd said Finn's name in years.

"To Finn," she echoed back. Strong and sure. Then finished her shot before Sawyer had even lifted his to his lips.

Huge mistake? she thought as she sucked on the lemon slice and looked right into Sawyer's beautiful blue eyes, joy now flooding into all the places her earlier concern had resided.

And that was the final thought she remembered having for some time.

CHAPTER TWO

MONDAY MORNING, dressed in her favourite dark caramel jumpsuit, an autumnal-toned floral jacket and her lucky high-heeled aubergine boots—lucky because she'd been wearing them when a certain crooner had called her *personally* to beg she deck out his Aspen chalet—Petra dropped off her dry-cleaning on her way to her first day at her new job.

Only to find herself stuck, as the woman behind the counter was impressed by what she called the "uber-rummy scent" of one of Petra's dresses.

"Not a rum drinker," Petra assured her.

The woman raised an eyebrow. "Daiquiri, mojito, piña colada, Mai Tai, Dark and Stormy?"

Petra's mouth popped open, ready to assure her otherwise, till she saw the dusky pink tulle and realised it was the dress she'd worn on Saturday night. Meaning she couldn't be sure.

She *thought* she remembered Deena dancing on someone's shoulders. And had there been *karaoke*? There were remnants of a deep and meaningful conversation with someone from the hen night crowd regarding whether it was wrong for a mother of three kids to see a film just because it starred Timothée Chalamet.

What she remembered most vividly, though, was Sawyer. Hugging him so hard she could feel his imprint along her entire body, dusting his nose with a swipe of her finger, curling her hand through his arm and leaning into his meaty shoulder.

But the rest? Not so much.

So Petra merely smiled, asked when her dry-cleaning might be ready, then with big dark sunglasses in place to ward off the last lingering vestiges of Saturday night ickiness she went in search of a hearty breakfast.

Belly full, hot coffee warming her hands, only then did she switch off the Do Not Disturb function on her watch. Her wrist buzzed immediately.

For a second her heart leapt, imagining it might be *him*.

Sawyer had messaged her the day before.

Morning. Hope your head's okay.

She'd assured him it was not, returned a laughing emoji and that was that.

Maybe this time he was calling to ask when they could catch up again. Since they were both in town. At the same time. For a bit.

But no.

Petra found her phone in her bag and read the full message.

DARLING!

Her mother again, with the caps lock on.

ASSUMING YOU'RE ON YOUR WAY TO WORK? FIRST DAY... GOOD IMPRESSION... A REMINDER THAT DISCRETION IS PARAMOUNT. THE GALLERY'S REPUTATION DEPENDS ON IT!

Petra considered using caps lock back, then reminded herself that passive aggression was not her favourite thing. So she typed:

On my way! Ready and raring! Can't wait!

Then, feeling as if she were about to get a sugar toothache, she tossed her phone back in her bag. This trip had better improve things between them, or they were doomed to play out the Ingenuous Daughter/Disappointed Parent dynamic for ever. And, well, they were now all one another had.

One last quick check of her phone in case she'd missed any important messages—aka any from Sawyer—then Petra grabbed her coffee and made her way down the hill towards the gallery.

Where she planned to magically figure out how to beg for money, from people who didn't know her, in as timely a manner as possible, while not scandalising anyone, or thinking of Sawyer Mahoney much at all.

Around an hour before opening time Petra showed her ID to the lovely old security guard. Before heading up to the admin floor she made a quick trek to the heart of the gallery—the *Then and Now* exhibition, an impressive array of classic Australian art, including a familiar-looking Sidney Nolan painting.

"On loan from the collection of the Gilpin family," she read off the plaque on the wall. It brought with it an unexpected wave of nostalgia.

Petra's big brother Finn had been the golden child. And fully deserved too, for he'd been handsome, smart, funny, athletic and a dauntless extrovert. Exactly the kind of child that well-to-do go-getters like Josiah and Josephine would expect.

Petra, on the other hand, had been dreamy and quiet and odd. The one thing they'd seen eye to eye on was art.

And once they'd realised they couldn't convince Finn to give a jot about painting, Petra had become their go-to companion at any gallery event, given tacit permission to wander freely through the basement collections, and the restoration floor, while her parents did whatever they did to help keep the place running.

The clearing of a throat from a security guard

somewhere nearby had Petra shaking off the bittersweets, lifting her chin and making a beeline for the lifts leading to the administrative floor.

Her relief when the lift doors opened was immediate. Behind the scenes, in the messy hustle, was where she belonged.

Petra meandered around big peeling pylons decorated with layers of posters stuck over one another, wrapped in fake ivy and fairy lights, under an amazing domed skylight letting in the weak Melbourne sunshine.

She noted the *many* empty desks, the piles of merchandising material yet to be stored, or tossed. And thought it looked as if they were still moving in. Or in the process of moving out.

In the far corner, according to the information her mother had sent, was HER OFFICE. Petra had been told it would be READY TO USE, so had imagined a utilitarian desk, a chair, a phone. An elegant jail cell.

Imagine her surprise at finding a wall of fantastically rugged exposed brick covered in framed pictures of all the special collections she'd attended as a child. Add a funky cream leather office chair, big blond wood desk, pink blanket thrown over the back of the comfy-looking caramel-coloured sofa and a kidney-shaped coffee table boasting a vase of fresh pink peonies.

Her mother's attempt at making it Petra-friendly? Her intuition hiccupped in surprise.

When her watch buzzed she looked at it through a single squinted eye, in case she was attacked by capital letters, only to find a message from Sawyer.

You've got this.

Grinning, she grabbed her phone and typed back.

Heck, yeah, I do!

"Ms Gilpin!"

Petra looked up to find a petite brunette in over-sized glasses standing at her office door. "Hi?"

The young woman swept into the room, leant over the desk and held out a hand. "Firstly, I have to tell you I am such a huge fan. I've watched the video tour of that rapper's ranch a zillion times. The collection you curated is the reason I tacked a fine arts minor onto my business degree."

"Wow. Thank you," said Petra, honestly taken aback. Being a curator meant she was the one behind the art that went into the homes of the kind of people who had fans.

"I'm Mimi, by the way. Your assistant. At least I'd like to be considered for the role."

Petra crossed her legs and sat back. "Do I not already have an assistant?"

Mimi grimaced. "As far as the whispers around here go, you're on your own."

Petra felt a moment of surprise, before she

coughed out a laugh. Beautiful office space, but no help. That sounded about right. "May I ask how you survived the redundancies?"

Mimi said, "I'd only been here for three days when it all went down."

"Three *days*?"

Mimi grimaced. "I know, right? My dream job and *whoomph*. Up in smoke before I'd even figured out how to use the coffee machine."

Petra tapped her fingers on her desk. "Figured it out yet?"

Mimi grinned. "Test me."

"Big. Strong. Whisper of milk."

"Coming right up."

Mimi bolted from the room, though she took a moment first to tap something into the computer on the desk just outside Petra's office. "Check your email!" she shouted before hustling off, presumably to make coffee.

Petra pulled her laptop from her bag, turned it on, trailed a finger over the mousepad, to find a message from the desk of Mimi Lashay, Interim Assistant to Petra Gilpin.

Mimi with the Business Degree and Fine Arts Minor had put together a thorough portfolio of the gallery's legacy benefactors, including those who'd lapsed, and made a list of Melbourne's untapped up-and-comers, entitled *Legacy*, *Lapsed* and *Opportunities Missed*.

And Petra wondered which gods she had to thank for Mimi Lashay.

She opened the file and went straight to the latter section. The unexpected was much more her bag than the establishment.

Right up at the top—alongside corresponding accolades, awards, titles and articles, including one entitled *Top Ten Sexiest Single Billionaire Bachelors Under Forty* and an estimate of individual net worth boasting a staggering number of zeroes—were three names she recognised in an instant.

Ronan Gerard, Ted Fincher and Sawyer Mahoney. The co-founders of Big Think Corp.

Petra burst into laughter.

One thing she remembered, for sure, about Saturday night was deciding *not* to ask Sawyer for a donation. The lines of their friendship were blurry enough without giving him explicit permission to go all knight in shining armour.

Though she did take a minute to read Mimi's report before moving on—Mimi had put so much effort into it after all—and quickly found herself flabbergasted at how deep, how wide, their interests ran. Including, hilariously, full ownership of the Gilded Cage, which explained Ronan's choice of location.

With their resources and investments, Big Think could accede and become their own nation.

"Big. Strong. Whisper of milk!"

Petra's hand lifted off her keyboard as if caught watching porn, only to find Mimi carefully placing the hot coffee on her desk, her eyes on the Big Think page.

"You should totally start there," Mimi said, nodding giddily.

"You think?" Petra said noncommittedly.

"Have you *seen* those guys?" Mimi pulled out her phone and fiddled with the thing, then turned to show Petra a photo of Ted, Ronan and Sawyer in tuxedos at some benefit or another. "They're like a real-life *GQ* spread."

"Mmm…" Petra mmmmed.

"So, the dark frowny one," said Mimi, pointing at Ronan. "His family are off-the-charts wealthy. If we could convince him to flick us his fun money allowance, we'd be golden."

Fun money allowance? Petra hid her laughter behind her coffee as she imagined making that call.

"And the redhead, the big guy in the glasses." Mimi pointed at the picture of Ted Fincher, who Petra had never met. "He's like this amazing science brain. The projects he has in the works, the patents, the tests—game-changing!"

And there was Sawyer: grinning, clean-shaven, so beautiful it hurt to look at him. "What about the last one?" Petra asked, going for nonchalant.

"That's Sawyer Mahoney. He used to be this superstar AFL player. When I was five I had a jersey with his number on the back. My mum claims I cried for a week when he broke his leg. He never played again."

Petra understood Mimi's young crush all too well. "Great job. Honestly."

Mimi grinned and said, "I'll be at my desk if you need me."

Leaving Petra to swing back and forth on her office chair. And think.

Old money, venerable benefactors, dusty family names—that was how the art world had flourished for a long time. That was her parents in a nutshell.

Whereas Petra was most in demand with musicians, movie execs, crypto success stories, influencers, mumpreneurs. If she could find a way to tap into *that* audience, they might not be dead in the water.

Movement outside her office. More staff were arriving. If Mimi was right, they didn't belong to her. But their jobs still depended on whether or not she could fix the gallery's problems.

Considering the place had not changed a bit since she'd last been there—the same tired displays, same stale heritage wall colours, same scent of antediluvian dust on the back of the tongue—she feared its problems ran deeper than mere funding.

Meaning she needed to get cracking.

Only she couldn't get Sawyer Mahoney out of her head.

She grabbed her phone, pressed call, lent back in her very nice chair and propped her feet up on her very nice desk.

"Mahoney," he answered.

"Sawyer, hi." A hand on her belly to settle the instant swoop, then, "It's Petra."

"Hey," he said, and she felt the deepening of his voice like a fingertip tracing her spine. A few seconds beat past, then the call sounded different. As if he'd pressed the phone closer to his ear. Or closed a door. "Everything okay?"

"Brilliant!" she said, her voice overbright. "You?"

"I'm fine. But I didn't absorb a bottle of tequila on Saturday night."

"Half a bottle," she shot back. For he'd had the other half. Hadn't he? Like an echo, or an echo of an echo, she heard a Kylie song in her head.

It disappeared as Sawyer said, "If you're worried about the picture, Ronan's Doberman of an assistant, Hadley, is on it."

"What picture?"

Silence.

"Sawyer! You can't say something like that then leave me hanging!"

"There's a picture circulating. From the other night."

"Of me?" Petra asked, the words *whiff of scandal* kicking about inside her head.

"Of us."

The Kylie song was back, stronger this time, and Petra's instincts flickered like a pilot light on a cold night. Not quite awake, but stirring. As if there *was* something about Saturday night that she knew she ought to remember. Or was best left forgotten.

"What were we doing?" she asked, now madly typing her name and Sawyer's into the search bar on her laptop, but nothing came up. Nothing new anyway. Only old youth football images from when Finn and Sawyer played together.

"Nothing," Sawyer said. "Just talking."

"Right. Of course." As if they'd ever do anything else! "Is that a concern?"

"Not for me. You, on the other hand, mentioned quite a few times that *what happens at the Gilded Cage stays at the Gilded Cage.* So I was concerned *you* might be concerned."

"Ahh!" Deena's maxim must have made an impact after all. Though... "My mother did make a bit of a big deal about not wanting even a *whiff of scandal* surrounding my appointment. Due to some old behind-the-scenes stuff. So maybe that was on my mind?"

"Right," he said, his voice dropping into protector mode. "Do you want me to continue with the cease and desist?"

"No! That sounds extreme."

She'd been in plenty of press photos over the years. In the background, unnamed, untagged, mere ambience, like the décor she'd curated. "So long as they caught my good side."

A beat. Then, "Which is your good side?"

"Isn't it obvious?"

Another beat, that stretched into several. As if Sawyer knew it was a trap. Which it totally was.

Then, "Sorry, Petra, can you excuse me for a sec?"

"Sure."

The phone muffled as if Sawyer had put his hand over the microphone and she heard his deep voice as he spoke to someone.

Petra tapped her finger against her mouth, popped the call onto speaker, then checked her social media notifications. Bingo! She'd been tagged in a story.

She opened it to find a glaringly bright, colourful image of a bunch of young women in pink veils, the hen night group from the Gilded Cage. And in the background, nibbling on a thumbnail and frowning at her phone was *@petrart*.

How on earth had they found her handle? *Deena*. At the edge of the photo, holding up a glass of bubbly and grinning for all she was worth.

Petra tapped through the rest of the stories. Lots of dancing and toasting. Photos of disco balls and clinking glasses.

A 'who has the longest arm' selfie with a bunch of faces crammed into the shot.

Petra held a finger to the screen, so that the image paused.

For in the background, paying them no heed, she and Sawyer faced one another at the bar. No tag this time, pure coincidence.

Her hand hovered near his chest, her hair tumbled wildly down her back as her face was tipped up to his, the tulle of her skirt lifted as her knee was cocked his way. She could feel the warm crush of the crowd and a heady looseness in her body. Could feel her happiness in that moment with a kind of dizzying assurance.

Then, just before she lifted her finger, she noted his knee was cocked too. In fact, it was touching hers—

"You there?" Sawyer asked.

"Yep!" she squeaked, swiping the story off her screen.

"Was there a reason you called?"

Apart from needing to hear his voice, she could put him out of her head and get on with her day? "I have a question about the other night."

A pause, then, "All right."

"Did we drink rum?"

A beat, then a bark of laughter, as if he'd been holding his breath. As if he'd been expecting her to ask something else.

"No," he said, before she could imagine what that something might be. Then, "There was tequila. And champagne. Though what you got up to with Deena, and those rowdy hen night girls, before I finally poured you into a taxi, I can't be sure."

Oh. So he'd stuck around, dusty and jet-lagged as he'd been, waiting till she was done for the night. Which ought to have made her growl, considering the whole little sister thing, but instead it made her feel…safe. Made her feel valued.

"Let's have lunch," she said.

"Lunch."

"It's a meal some people enjoy in the middle of the day. I'm thinking I order a salad, steal chips from your plate and make jokes about how much you need a haircut."

Sawyer laughed, a rough-edged hum that did things to her insides that were wholly unfair.

"How's the Elysium sound? Around one."

"Sure," she said, jotting down a note to find out where the heck the Elysium was.

"See you then." He hung up.

And Petra let out a lusty sigh.

A knock at her door, then, "Ms Gilpin?"

Mimi sure knew how to interrupt a daydream. Which, to be fair, happened a lot in the land of Petra. Meaning, this might already be the most perfect relationship she'd ever had.

"What's up?" Petra asked.

"Need another coffee?"

"No. Thank you. But do you want to drag a chair in here and we can work on the Opportunities Missed list together?"

Mini nodded. Ran out of the room. Grabbed

her chair, dragged it in and sat. Tablet and stylus at the ready. "So, we ditch the legacy list?"

A small part of her wanted to say yes. To prove, in a big way, that she and her kind, her ways, had merit. But this place was bigger than her.

"Art isn't about gilt frames," Petra said. "It's not about provenance or exclusivity. It's about exploration and empathy, connection and revelation. It bravely leaves itself wide open to interpretation and judgement, from and for everyone. So we won't leave any avenue unexplored when it comes to ensuring its survival."

Mimi said, "Find more donors."

And Petra knew she'd found her assistant. "One more thing."

"Yes, Ms Gilpin?"

"Call me Petra."

They spent the next hour coming up with lists of influencers and young artists and designers and creatives.

When Mimi went back to her desk, Petra grabbed her phone, found the earlier tag, saved the picture of her and Sawyer to her camera roll, before tossing her phone into her bag with only a mild case of self-disgust.

Sawyer flipped his phone, with its beat-up case, back and forth between his hands, a smile tugging at his mouth, a frown pulling at his forehead.

Petra Gilpin, blithely befuddling him for half a lifetime.

He'd been thinking of her all morning, hoping she was settling in okay. On Saturday night, he'd been given a detailed rundown as to the many reasons why she wished she'd not taken on the job.

Then Hadley—Ronan's executive assistant— had sent him the photo, something she liked to do when any of the three of them were photographed in any way that had not been sanctioned by her.

Yes, the photo was innocuous. And, so far, isolated. But Ted had put himself squarely in the firing line a number of months earlier, having taken up with the journalist writing a feature story on him. Ted *did* end up marrying Adelaid, and having a daughter – reaching peak of wholesomeness Hadley was still twitchy.

Sawyer was not interested in Hadley's twitches. His sole interest was to make sure Petra was okay.

Liar, growled a voice in the back of his head.

He growled back.

Fine, so he was also still working his way through all that had gone down at the club. Not that anything had *gone down*. Not really. But he had been...unnerved.

Could have been the surprise at seeing her.

Could also have been the shock of realising just how much time had passed. Last time they'd been together she'd been a dreamy, soft-spoken eighteen-year-old. Saturday night's Petra had been all wild waves and a kind of magnetic self-awareness.

It didn't help that the club had been so packed they'd had to stand danger close all night long. That she'd kept lifting onto her toes to speak into his ear, her breath brushing over his neck again and again and again. As for her story about Russell—

Sawyer shut his eyes tight. Nope. He was not going to think about Russell. Ever again.

Now, it seemed—considering the rum query— that *she* didn't remember all that had gone down. Not that anything *had* gone down. Not really.

But maybe it was best it stayed that way. They could put a line under Saturday night and move on.

Using the murmur of voices on the other side of the hallway wall as a lifeline, Sawyer ducked through the doorway of the near-mythical Big Think Founders' Room they'd allotted for themselves when designing the fancy-schmancy new Big Think Tower. Anyone outside the group would be dismayed to find it looked—and sometimes smelled—a heck of a lot like the university lounge in which they'd first become friends.

Sawyer opened the door to find Hadley standing darkly in the doorway. He swore, all but tripping backwards over himself to avoid smacking into her.

Ted looked up from his spot on the dilapidated old blue lounger that used to belong to his dad,

then back at the research paper he'd been anno-
tating.

Ronan barely spared him a glance from what
looked like a throne at the head of the table. "Finally ready to join us, Mahoney?"

Sawyer rubbed discreetly at his leg. Specifically, the scar tissue beneath which pins held his
leg together. Then he narrowed his eyes at Hadley, before giving her a dramatically wide berth.

"A lot to get through," Ronan drawled. "Considering how long it's been since we were all in
the same room."

Knowing that was a dig at him for taking an
extra few weeks at the end of his last trip. But
the chance to work one-on-one with actual communities, actual people, rather than committees,
or governments, or bureaucrats he was assigned
to, had been too rewarding to pass up.

Though, as per usual, having taken a rare
chance to do something for himself, he was now
paying for it.

"Begin away," Sawyer allowed magnanimously.
Straddling a chair, he grabbed a handball from
the bowl that lived permanently on the table for
his use.

"Hadley?" Ronan demanded.

Hadley glared at Ronan for a moment before
turning to Sawyer. "Any idea how long you'll be
in town this time?"

Sawyer thought of his mum's phone calls, her

growing concerns for his youngest sister, Daisy. The weight of familial responsibility that had finally tugged him home.

Then he thought of Petra. Her insistence they have lunch.

"For a bit," he said.

"Excellent," said Hadley. "The Big Think Ball is coming up in a few months, so this is prime schmooze time. We don't need any antics that will pull focus. Ted has been forced to pull your weight, Mahoney, so you're going to make up for it."

"Suits me," said Ted, offering a thumbs-up.

Sawyer rubbed his leg again.

Not that it hurt. More a phantom echo. One that seemed to appear any time he was forced to smile and wave and stick to the neat and tidy Big Think origin story.

Of course he was grateful to have broken his leg playing footy. Otherwise he'd never have learnt about the disparity in rehab between the haves and have-nots, which had sent him back to university to study Social Work and International Relations. Which was how he'd met doctorate student Ted Fincher and MBA candidate Ronan Gerard.

Not that he had any intention of sharing the other moments in his life that had brought him to that point.

"Why do they call you the brawn of Big Think? Is that a reference to your football days?"

"My dad died when I was eight, making me the man of the house, so doing what has to be done is the only way I know how to be."

"And what motivated you to be such a fierce competitor? If you'd played with a little less vigour, might you have saved your sporting career?"

"I broke my leg playing footy; my best friend broke his neck. I was lucky, while Finn, at nineteen, had barely begun to grow into his own possibilities. Since that day I've felt it my duty to achieve enough for the both of us."

Not that he believed either of those happenstances were his fault. But his literal job, on the team, was to be the hard man, protecting Finn's flights on the wing. How could he not help wondering: what if he'd been there that day, rather than off on a representative footy camp? Would it have happened at all?

Sawyer grabbed another ball, juggled them with one hand.

"Can you commit to all of this?" Hadley asked, holding up her tablet.

Sawyer looked up, realised she was talking to him.

"Have you been paying attention at all?" Hadley asked.

"Some." He grinned, the kind that distracted. "I'm assuming you each gave a speech, in thanks, as to how much I achieved in Big Think's name these past months. Then apologised for being so slow at doing your bit and giving more world-saving projects to go out there and hawk."

Ted grinned, Ronan muttered under his breath, and Hadley snorted. Then death-stared him for daring to make her succumb to such indignity.

"You assumed wrong," Hadley said.

"Ah. Then, till then I'm yours to wield as you see fit. Except—" said Sawyer.

"Here we go," Ronan grumbled.

"Except lunchtime today. I'm busy."

"Doing what?" Hadley asked, frowning at her tablet.

"Having lunch." Sawyer tossed a ball and caught it behind his back. "With Petra."

At that Ronan's gaze finally lifted. "Petra *Gilpin*?" For Ronan and Petra had known one another as kids, running in the same Brighton rich kid circle.

Hadley said, "I'm assuming this is the same Petra Gilpin with whom you were photographed in a nightclub looking like a caveman who'd slept in a cement factory. Said photo you want taken down under threat of death and dismemberment."

"About that," said Sawyer, clicking his fingers at Hadley. "Turns out it's not a problem after all."

Hadley rolled her eyes before tapping at her tablet, likely sending a directive to whichever shadowy figure or family member of hers took care of such things.

Ronan tapped his fingers on the desk. "Petra is doing well for herself these days. Her parents are old money. And none of them are Big Think benefactors. Romance her at lunch. See if she or her parents might come on board."

Sawyer tossed the ball again, but he missed completely. The thing bounced off the table, then off at an angle, just missing Ted, before landing in a pot plant in the corner.

He had zero intention of *romancing* Petra. Protecting her, the way her brother would have, had he still been around; that was his purview where she was concerned.

Hadley swept her stylus over her tablet and Sawyer's battered old phone buzzed on the table. "Your calendar is now updated."

He hopped out of the chair when his leg began to hurt for real, and moved to a spare couch along the back wall. Twisting to lie back, his feet on the opposite armrest, he continued to toss the ball.

Till the familiarity of the banter, the mind-boggling ideas thrown about, the determination in that room to actually make a difference, settled over him like a warm blanket.

For it was a rare room in which he could justly share the weight of responsibility and didn't feel the burning duty to shoulder all. Only because the people in that room wouldn't have allowed him in otherwise.

CHAPTER THREE

"I'D FORGOTTEN HOW wild Melbourne traffic can be. And I lived near the Arc de Triomphe for two years," said Petra, as she dropped her big soft bag onto the table and flumped dramatically into the chair across from Sawyer.

Sawyer said nothing, for he was still coming out of the fog that had descended over him at the sight of her sweeping into the restaurant, all long and loose and so comfortable in her own skin she shone with it.

"How's your first day so far?" he asked.

"Strange," she said, "but not terrible. How about you? Ronan as painful as ever?"

"More so with every passing year."

"Ha." She gave him another quick smile, before looking around the hotel restaurant. No doubt clocking the stark white walls, the neon art, the chunky composition which was as natural to her as breathing.

"What do you think?" he asked.

"It's…sunny."

He laughed, for she sounded as if she was making polite noises regarding his hovel under a park bridge. It was refreshing to find that although Petra had taken herself out of Melbourne, you couldn't quite take the Gilpin out of her. Not that she'd want to hear that.

Then she was flicking through her phone, before sliding it across the table. "I found the photo's origin, by the way—the one from the other night. One of the hen night girls put it on her Instagram."

Sawyer looked, jaw clenching. For it wasn't, in fact, the same picture at all.

The one Hadley had sent him had been much closer, taken over Petra's shoulder. A deliberate shot taken of him, looking, as Hadley had pointed out, more caveman than billionaire philanthropist.

This one, while incidental, was far more provocative. The way they curled towards one another, her hand pressed against his chest, their knees touching. Anyone seeing this image would be forgiven for thinking they were moments from—

Nothing. Nothing had happened. So it wasn't even worth considering.

Sawyer handed back the phone. "If it concerns you, I can still do something about it. We have ways and means."

"Like what?"

"The blushing bride?" He mimed a finger slicing across his throat.

Petra barked out a laugh, her mouth wide, her

eyes sparking devilishly. And while it felt so familiar, so her, it hit him just how much she'd changed, her gentle sweetness having morphed into effortless cool.

"Not necessary," she said, before looking to her phone for a moment, her tongue darting out to wet her lower lip, before she put it away.

"Now, I have a bone to pick with you." She waggled a finger at him. "Why didn't you tell me you own the Gilded Cage?"

Sawyer sat back in his seat, glad to have moved on. "I did."

"When?"

"Saturday night. Some time between 'Copacabana' and 'Raspberry Beret'."

She blinked at him, clearly trying to remember the moment. But, as he'd expected, her memory was patchy.

"And you own *this* place too," she said accusingly. "I looked it up."

"Big Think does, yes."

Petra pointed a thumb over her shoulder. "Is that why there's a photographer in the bushes outside?"

The hairs rose on the back of Sawyer's neck and his feet flattened against the floor. "Did he bother you? Is he still out there, do you think?"

"What? No!" She held up both hands in surrender. "I mean, he kind of looked like a tourist in his khakis and matching puffer jacket, so he was probably just taking a photo of the hotel and I got in the way."

Maybe. But maybe not. People taking photos of him was one thing, anyone making Petra feel uncomfortable was quite another.

"Drink?" Petra asked, changing the subject and catching the attention of a passing waiter.

She asked for a particular brand of iced tea, it was pink. It made Sawyer smile. So he ordered the same.

After the waiter left, her smile turned down at the corners. "What? Is there something on my face?"

Caught staring, Sawyer leant in, stared harder. "Just reconciling the Petra sitting before me with Petra at fourteen. You and your pink feathers, and stones, and sea glass and whatnot. You had bowls of the stuff all over the house."

She flicked her napkin and laid it across her lap, then lifted narrowed eyes his way. "I like what I like."

"That much was clear."

"To you, maybe," she said.

"It was," he reiterated, aware that her parents had favoured her brother. "Though fourteen-year-old Petra was a girl of compelling contradictions. Off with the fairies one minute and screaming at footy umpires if they did me wrong the next."

Petra's eyes widened, as if surprised he'd noticed. It had been hard not to, for she'd been the third musketeer, always around. When not yelling at umpires, she'd been so unruffled—by Finn's boisterousness, or her parents' vexation. Coming from his crazy house, with his loud sisters and despairing mother, her sweet unflappability had been a balm.

"Then you turned fifteen," he said, "and began sighing moodily over paintings by... Who was it? Caravaggio?"

At that, Petra leant her chin on her hand and batted her lashes. "All those men with their big muscles and sweaty limbs. Their faces, twisted in pleasure."

"Pain," Sawyer said, his throat a little tight. "I think you'll find their faces were twisted in pain."

"Same-same," she said, before she turned and smiled at the waiter who'd brought their drinks.

Allowing Sawyer to breathe out. Hard. And shift on his seat.

Petra ordered her salad, and for Sawyer steak and chips.

"Charge it to room 1201," he said, before the waiter nodded and left.

"What? You're actually staying *here*?" said Petra. "In a *hotel*?"

"I believe we just established that it's a very nice hotel."

"I'm sure, but—"

"Twenty-four-hour room service. A dozen cabanas by the pool. Award-winning design. And the beds are like sleeping on a cloud."

"I'll take your word for it."

An innocent response, and yet something flashed between them. A spark. Some acknowledgement that time and distance had both of them seeing one another with fresh eyes.

Then she levelled him with a look that was pure Petra. "Unlike me, *you* actually live in Melbourne. And I know you can afford it, Mr Big Shot. If you didn't fork out for houses for your entire family the moment you could, I'll eat my boots. And these are my lucky boots. So, what gives?"

"I travel more than I don't, so I don't see the point."

"Where's all your stuff?"

"What stuff?"

She coughed and spluttered, as if unable to compute the thought of living out of a suitcase permanently. "Your stuff! Your things, your treasures, your memories. Your art!"

"I think we established my eye for art is less than exemplary."

"Rubbish. If you know when something feels beautiful to you, then you understand art."

Another moment of eye-contact, another spark.

Sawyer squinted towards the bar. "An unused house is surplus to requirements. Nothing but a big dust-collector. A blight on the environment."

"Mmm," she said, unable to curb her smile as she sipped at her pink drink through a striped paper straw.

"So where are *you* staying?" he asked. "With Josiah and Josephine?"

Petra choked on her drink. "Apartment in the city," she eventually managed. "A six month lease."

"I bet it's nice."

Her mouth twitched, a delicate arc flashing at one corner. "It's getting there. Two bedrooms. Two bathrooms. Too big really, for one person. In fact—"

She stopped and came to a conclusion he ought to have seen coming.

"Stay with me!" she said.

"We're a little old to play sleepover, don't you think?"

"Seriously, the apartment is huge. It's fully furnished. I have a cleaner. Groceries delivered every three days. I'll be working a lot, so you'd barely see me."

"You say that as if it's a selling point." Yeah, even he heard the note of dissent in his voice with that one.

And again that spark seemed to flash between them. Like a crackle of lightning forming in mid-air.

"We *never* see one another anyway, Sawyer. The fact that we are both here now, it feels like serendipity. Don't you think?"

He did think. He just wasn't sure that was what he should be thinking.

"You *just* said I'd never see you," he said, prevaricating.

"Ignore what I said. I'm riffing here."

Sawyer laughed. Only a Gilpin would consider a real estate deal riffing.

"No pool cabanas, but the showers are phenomenal. Both rainforest and wall-mounted heads. With several settings. Not that I've tried them all out," she said, before he had the chance to go there. Then, with a very grown-up grin, followed up with, "Only because I haven't had the time."

And, just like that, Russell popped into his mind.

Dammit. He'd tried really hard to forget there was a Russell. Without even the slightest measure of success. Another reason why staying with her would *not* be a good idea.

She plucked her oversized bag from the table and pulled out a set of keys, slipped one free and slid it across to him. "I'll text you the address and let Security know I'll have a guest."

"Petra," he warned, overwhelmingly sure that he needed to simply say no.

"Come on!" she said. "You can be my guard-dog. Any robbers scouting the street would take one look at you, with your battered jacket and all your tats, and this new bad boy beard you have going on, and they'd move on fast."

Sawyer's back teeth ground. Did she know she'd just pulled out the single reason why he'd agree to such a scenario? The knowledge he'd be right there if anything happened.

"I'll think about it," he growled.

"Brilliant. Now, is it warm in here or is it just me?" she said, sliding her floral jacket free and laying it over the back of her chair.

No, Sawyer thought, it wasn't just her. The spark had found kindling, the temperature only rising as Petra lifted her hair from her neck before twirling it over one shoulder.

Sawyer deliberately racked focus, only to find she was wearing the thin gold necklace Finn had given her one Christmas.

He knew as he'd helped pick it out…

"Rose gold."

"What now?" Finn asked as they stood outside the jewellery store.

"She'd like the rose gold."

Heat crept up Sawyer's neck as Finn looked at him as if he were speaking another language.

"It's kind of pink. Look."

He gave Finn a shove and pointed in the direction of three necklaces draped over a puffy velvet pillow—one normal gold, one silver and one rose gold.

"Oh, yeah! You're right."

Finn put him in a headlock before they shuffled inside.

"Where would I be without you?"

Sawyer blinked, his chest tight, uncomfortably so, as he looked up to find two girls in their late teens linking elbows and staring at him.

"It's not him!" said one. "He doesn't have a beard. And he's not that old."

"You're Sawyer Mahoney, right?" said the other.

Sawyer thought about telling them no. With the beard, a random accent, he could probably fake his way out of it. Then he remembered Hadley and her rabid insistence they play extra nice till the Big Think Ball.

He said, "So, I've been told."

"Told you! Can we, like, have a selfie?" said one.

"Her mum *loves* you," said the other.

Petra snorted from the other side of the table.

One of the girls was already leaning in towards him and holding her phone at arm's length up high in the air. "She'll totally scream when she hears we met you."

A few click-click-clicks and they were done.

One of the girls jerked back when she noticed belatedly that Sawyer had company. To Petra she said, "Are you somebody?"

Petra waved her hands madly and said, "Not even slightly."

"Okay. Well, thanks!" And with that the girls bounced off, giggling and checking their phones.

Petra squinted at him. "Is *that* normal for you?"

"It comes in waves. And usually only when I'm home."

She leant her chin on her hand, no batting lashes this time. "So when you're *not* here you have anonymity. That must be a relief. Unless you *love* the fawning fans. The sighing girls. The adoring mums."

"It's a hardship, but I cope."

"Mmm. So if we keep hanging out, what *are* the chances of getting through drinks or dinner without someone taking your photo?"

"Slim to fair."

"Meaning I might end up in more photos that give Hadley hives."

"Chances are."

She looked at him for a long while then, her mouth twisting side to side. "So long as you don't rob a bank, or trip an old lady, or say 'art sucks' while with me, then I can't see any problem with the world knowing we are friends."

Not his best friend's little sister, and her big brother's best friend. Friends of their own accord. Surely he could handle that too.

Then she looked at him as if it was her turn to reconcile Sawyer at sixteen with the man before her now.

He'd been knackered by then, working two

jobs, playing footy any chance he had, when not looking after his mum and sisters.

But he'd also been *sixteen*, and fuelled by hot air and ambition. Determined to be scouted by an AFL team. Family folklore telling tales of how his dad had nearly made it to the big leagues, but not quite. While also quietly hoping that life might give him an out. A chance to carve out his own niche.

He didn't realise he was rubbing his leg till his knuckles cracked with the effort.

"How do you cope?" Petra asked.

"With?"

"Attention. Photographers. Fans. People telling you how amazing you are all the time. The pressure. The *judgement*."

Sawyer ran a hand up the back of his neck, to find he really could do with a haircut. "I engage, but don't encourage. I smile, take the photo and thank them, as if it was my idea. I never deny any accusation, no matter how wacky, as my denial will become the story. You want to control your own narrative as much as you can. Do all that and it's over sooner rather than later."

"You could just tell them to eff off."

Sawyer laughed. "I could. If not for the very real fear Hadley would have my guts for garters."

Petra grinned. "You're a saint. Are you even real?"

"Pinch me," he said, holding out an arm, "and I'll let you know."

She didn't pinch him. Or even deign to glance down. Neither did he, caught as he was by the slight hook at the corner of her mouth. The humour in her eyes.

When they'd done nothing but look into one another's eyes for a few seconds, she broke into a grin. Then a bout of breathy laughter. Patently glad to be with him.

He wanted to tell her how good it was to see her again. How much he'd missed her lightness, her smile, her ease. Missed the way she'd never wanted anything from him bar his company. A quality he'd not realised was so rare, how precious, till now.

Then their food arrived, the steak steaming, the salad gleaming. And the moment was gone.

Later that evening, after sending a zillion expressions of interest packages to their A-list of possible new donors, Petra turned the key in her apartment door. Slowly, quietly.

Then poked her head around the door and listened.

"Hello?"

No response. Meaning no Sawyer. Her heart sank.

She swung open the door, threw her keys, bag and tote containing the pack of pink fairy lights and the triptych of happy face paintings she'd picked up in a small shop on the way back to the apartment on the hall table. Then unzipped her aubergine boots, dragged them off one by one and let them fall where they may.

Twirling her hair into a messy bun and rubbing her neck, tight from spending so many hours behind an actual desk, she chose a playlist on her phone and cast it to a portable speaker, the music playing throughout the vast space taking the edge off the quiet.

Then, pulling a bottle of red from the fridge, she poured herself a glass and a half, pressed it to her cheek and stared into the fridge.

What had she been thinking? Asking Sawyer to stay with her. Expecting him to say yes!

Catching up some more would be fantastic. And just being in the same room as the man, for as long as she could have him, would fill her fantasy bank for a good long while.

But she wasn't back *for* him.

She was there to save a crumbling institution she now she feared was being mismanaged on multiple levels, all while proving to her parents that trusting her had been a good decision.

The last thing she needed was a distraction. And Sawyer was as big a distraction as she was likely to find.

Shutting the fridge door, the apartment grew

dark, the only light coming through the gauzy curtains covering the balcony doors.

Petra padded towards the view, opened the sliding door and stepped outside, a rush of cool evening air pressing against her, the lights of Melbourne twinkling back—

"Hey."

Petra cried out, sloshing her wine over the rim and spinning to find Sawyer splayed out in one of the outdoor chairs.

Jacket gone, he wore jeans and T-shirt, tattoos poking out under the edge of the sleeve and over his shoulders. One bare foot up on the table, hand gripping some battered paperback with the cover falling off. She could not have painted a hotter picture if she'd tried.

"Hi," she said, her voice breathless, her heart stammering in her chest.

"You okay?" he asked.

His instant protectiveness was enough to take the edge off, turning her attraction to the guy down from a strong eleven to a ten point five.

"Yep! Just didn't realise you were here."

He leaned forward, dropping both feet to the floor, taking up even more of the small space. "I mean your neck."

She was rubbing at it still, her fingers pressing deep. "I'm fine. Not used to sitting for so long."

"I give a mean massage," he offered.

Oh, she bet he did. But crushing on him from

a distance she could do. Had done, for ever. Massages, mean or otherwise, were a definite no-go zone.

Maybe she'd try out that fancy showerhead after all. On her neck. Yep, just her neck.

She let her hand drop and said, "So what did you do with the rest of your day?"

A quick frown, then a longer smile. "Visited home."

"How's your mum?"

"Good. Great, actually. Besotted with her grandkids. Though she thinks I need to take a break. Slow down."

Petra snorted. "You'd go off your tree if you didn't keep yourself busy."

A smile hooked at the corner of his mouth. "True."

Petra basked in the fact she knew him better than his own mother.

Sawyer kept smiling at her, while looking all warm and comfortable and delicious. And big and hot and tattooed. And—

"Nice nails," she blurted, in need of a subject change.

He knew it too, by the flicker of his mouth. But he let it go, wriggling his purple, glittery, messy toes as he said, "When I popped in to see Mum my sisters turned up within minutes. And everyone stayed for dinner."

Sawyer's family were a rowdy bunch. Rambunctious, noisy and really close. And they leaned on him like crazy. Had done after his dad died when he was really young. A little too much, from what she'd gathered, but she was hardly the expert when it came to healthy family dynamics.

"And how's Daisy?" Petra's favourite, bar Sawyer, of course.

"Not sure," he said, brow furrowing. "She wasn't there. She's proving to be hard to get a hold of."

"Right." From memory, Daisy had always been the black sheep of the Mahoney clan—creative, rebellious. "I remember her being a lot like me. She adores *you*. Keep trying, she'll relent."

Sawyer shot her a look, and it took her a moment to realise that the way she'd worded things she'd made it sound as if she adored him too. Which she did. She just had no intention of telling him so.

Petra turned away, leant against the balcony and said, "Pity she wasn't there, though. She'd have done a better job on that pedicure than your other sisters."

Sawyer laughed, the sound deep and rough and chaotic to her senses. "My five-year-old niece painted the left," he explained. "Four-year-old nephew painted the right."

"Sure sure," she said, glancing over her shoulder in time to catch a quick grin. The kind that came with canines, and a glint in those clear blue eyes.

"Did you find your room?" she asked, looking

back into the apartment. "Mine's the one closest to the kitchen."

"I figured it out."

Which was when Petra remembered—having left the apartment that morning not expecting company, she'd not thought to tidy up. Had she put her undies in the dirty clothes basket or were they draped over the end of her bed? Bed, for sure. Having grown up in a house that looked like something from a magazine she liked a little noise in her home, a little lived-in mess. And—

Oh, no. What about *Russell*? Awake crazy early, filled with nerves and the last vestiges of tequila, she'd brought him out that morning. Had she put him away? Too late now!

As for Sawyer's room—she'd have to avert her eyes any time she passed. The last thing she needed was to discover what kind of underwear *he* wore. Or to see his toothbrush leaning nonchalantly, intimately, in a glass on his sink.

Sawyer lifted an eyebrow slowly and she realised she was staring.

"So, you've eaten?" she asked, her voice peppy.

"I've eaten."

"Me too. Wine?"

"I'm good."

"Okay. Well, I'm going to—"

She was going to say *have a shower*, but thought better of it. She didn't need to imagine him imagining which showerhead setting she might use. Not that he would. Argh!

"I'm going to string up some lights I bought today, then head to my room to get some work done. Then sleep."

"'Night, Petra," Sawyer said.

"'Night, Sawyer," she said, then hotfooted it inside.

Reminding herself that as hot and delicious as he'd looked on her balcony, she had to be sensible here.

Sawyer had been the one constant through her life. Her biggest support. Her parents might never have understood her choices, but she had *someone* on her side. She couldn't mess with that. Couldn't lose that. For she wasn't sure who she'd be without it.

After finding places for the lights and the paintings, Petra downed her wine in one go, rinsed the glass and turned it upside down by the sink, before she hotfooted it into her room. Where she planned to stay till the next morning.

Some plans simply weren't meant to be.

"How is it that I heard from Deena Singh's aunt that you spent the night with Sawyer Mahoney?" Josephine Gilpin said by way of hello.

It took Petra a couple of seconds to make the connection.

Petra said, "I wasn't aware you knew Deena's aunt."

"It's late," her mother said on a sigh. "Humour me. Is it true?"

Petra rubbed her forehead. "Sawyer and I didn't *spend the night*...we bumped into one another a couple of nights ago. When I was out with Deena."

Letting her mother know he was asleep didn't feel necessary. Besides, her parents had always liked Sawyer. How could they not when he'd been so close to their son?

But there was a strange tightness in her mother's voice. Was it still about *Finn*? The same way Sawyer had baulked when she'd brought Finn up, her mother never talked about him. Ever. There was a pandemic of silence in the people around her. And it was not healthy.

Petra sat on the edge of her bed, curling her feet into the rug. "You know what? Finn's birthday is coming up soon. Maybe we can all—"

"Shoo. Shoo," her mother said. Then, "Honestly, those old man bike riders in their shiny Lycra. It's obscene. I've told your father that if he even thinks of taking it up, he can think again."

So much for that, then.

"Where are you?"

"In the car. On my way to the hospital." Where she'd been the head of Thoracic Surgery for the past fifteen years. "I'm on the Bluetooth. One of your father's old article clerks had to set it up for me."

Petra heard the words that had been left unsaid: *Because Finn's not here to do it.* Finn the tech whiz, as opposed to Petra, who'd spent her tech-learning years mooning over moody paintings by long-dead Dutchmen.

She ran a hand over her forehead. "So, quick update on the gallery. I have a great assistant named Mimi. We have a plan in place to lure fresh money—"

"We trust you have it all in hand."

Petra blinked. They did? Well, of course they did, or they'd not have asked for her help. It was just they'd never said anything of the sort. Out loud. To her.

Meaning maybe she should try one more time. "So, Finn's birthday—"

"I'm nearing the hospital. Must go."

Then Petra found herself on the end of a dead call as her mother hung up.

Wide awake now, Petra poked her head out of the bedroom door, waited till she was sure Sawyer wasn't around, then snuck into the lounge.

She switched on the fairy lights she'd bought that afternoon, smiled at the way the pink lights dappled her skin, a kitsch twist on the fantastical lighting in the Gilded Cage, and knew she'd use it in a show one day.

Lying back on the couch, TV on mute in the

background so as not to wake Sawyer, she read an article on her phone about a new local art prize, making notes on how the gallery might opt in.

Not imagining Sawyer in the spare room. Stretched out on the king-sized bed, wearing flannel PJs, or T-shirt and boxers—or nothing at all—tattooed arms akimbo, one knee cocked, the sheet draped just so—

"Hey," Sawyer's deep voice said from just behind her.

Petra screamed, arms flailing, the image she'd been building in her head exploding into glitter.

"You have to stop doing that!" she cried, cricking her neck to find him standing behind the couch. The blue light of the TV playing over his face, the T-shirt he'd worn earlier and his jeans, the top button unsnapped as if he'd only just pulled them on.

"Doing what?" Sawyer asked, his voice low, rusty, in the cool quiet of the night. Leaning to curl his hands over the back of the couch, right near her shoulder.

"Just…being there."

A raise of the eyebrows. "What happened to *'Stay with me, Sawyer…fight off the robbers for me, Sawyer'*?"

Petra coughed out a dumbfounded laugh, glad the darkness could hide the heat shooting up her neck. "For a big guy you have delicate footsteps, just saying."

"I have really good arches." He pushed away and padded slowly around the couch. "Back in the day, when my teammates were starting to suffer from collapsing arches, mine were perfect. Our team podiatrist used that exact word."

"Was she young? And female?"

Sawyer grinned, his teeth a flash of white in the low light.

Petra rolled her eyes.

"Thought you'd gone to bed," said Sawyer.

"Couldn't sleep. You?"

"Jetlag still playing havoc. I think."

In the quiet that followed, Petra considered heading back to her room. Tossing and turning till eventually she fell asleep. But she'd convinced him to stay with her, to spend time with her, so why not make the most of it?

"Sit," she said, pointing to the matching single-seater.

Sawyer either misread her instruction or ignored it and he moved to *her* couch, lifted her feet, sat and plonked her feet on his lap.

Her instincts buzzed, a little pre-warning warning. She told them to shush. She had this.

"What you watching?" he asked.

She somehow tore her gaze away from his big warm hands resting on her bare ankles to glance at the screen. "I wasn't watching; not really." Then, *"Camille Claudel."*

They watched in silence for a minute, his thumb

moving on her ankle, tracing the bone, before he asked, "What's it about?"

Art. French. Restrained desire and impossible attraction. She'd been obsessed with it in her teens. No two guesses as to why she'd felt a sudden nostalgic need to watch.

"Rodin," she said. "And his relationship with sculptor Claudel."

The only sounds in the room were their steady breaths, the occasional squeak of the couch and the hum of the fridge in the kitchen behind them.

Petra grabbed the remote and turned up the volume, and quickly found herself caught up in the language, the angst, the tension, the longing looks the leads shared on the screen.

"If you'd asked teenage me what I wanted to do with my life, I'd have said art school. But really, *that* was my dream."

"To sculpt?" Sawyer asked.

"To inspire."

Sawyer's hand stopped moving. She braved a look his way to find his eyes glued to the screen, his jaw tight. The night air felt thick around her.

Yeah, it was time to go to bed.

She made to move, to gather her feet towards her. Only Sawyer's thumb pressed into the arch of her foot. Finding the exact spot her favourite boots hurt by the end of a long day.

"This okay?" Sawyer asked, his gaze sweeping back to her, the usual clear blue all dark and smoky. "That same podiatrist taught me a trick or two."

"I bet she did."

Sawyer laughed softly, but did not, Petra noticed, deny the insinuation. Or stop massaging her foot. All intense, painful pleasure. The kind that hurt but you let it happen in the hopes it would soon feel so, so good.

His voice was low as he said, "My fourteen-year-old dream was to wake up and find one of my sisters had turned into a brother. Not quite so lofty as yours."

And Petra laughed, grateful to have been given a reprieve. "I loved having a big brother. Not sure Finn would have said the same about having me as a sister some of the time."

At that Sawyer stilled. And it felt as if all the air had been sucked from the room.

It had been such a long time since Finn's accident. Petra still felt the loss of him, for sure, but she'd chosen to take that empty space and fill it with all the best memories.

She'd long since wondered if Sawyer had filled this empty space by looking out for her.

She opened her mouth to address it somehow. To talk about Finn in a way that didn't make him flinch.

But then he pressed harder again, running his thumb along the pad of her foot. And every

.thought fled her head as she focused on the magic of his touch.

The movie played on. Sawyer's strong hands moved from her foot, to her ankle, then up her calf. And Petra let it happen.

Till Sawyer shifted, his body rolling against the couch, as if relieving some discomfort.

When she realised she'd braced her spare foot against his thigh, in the effort at keeping herself still, her eyes flickered open to find Rodin undressing Camille, her dress falling off one shoulder, his mouth tracing kisses along her collarbone.

She didn't have to glance at Sawyer to know he was watching it too. She could feel it in the sweep of his hands, moving in time with the vision on the TV.

It was so freaking sensual Petra could barely stand it.

And when he let her go, his hands reaching for her other foot, it was too much. She jerked away from the touch. The fact that she was so turned on her whole body hummed.

"You sure?" he asked. "You might walk funny if I don't even you up."

Yes, it was dark, and yes, it was night, but there was no mistaking the heat in his eyes. The way his nostrils flared as he dragged in a breath. And while she might dream that she was the one making it happen, she was well aware of the allure of nineties French cinema.

Slowly, lest he try to stop her, lest she let him, Petra dragged her feet over the crest of his hard thigh and onto her end of the couch.

"I'm sure. So tired," she said, feigning a yawn as she heaved herself to standing, her limbs a little shaky. "Shall I turn off the TV?"

Sawyer sank deeper into the couch, hitching his jeans in a way that had Petra's mouth watering. "I'm invested now. Got to see how it ends."

She considered telling him Claudel was later committed after exhibiting signs of paranoia— aka accusing Rodin of stealing her work—but instead went with, "It's French. If you like a happy ending, keep your expectations low."

His grin felt real. Like a gift. Then he held out his fingers to give them a stretch as if he too could still feel her skin beneath their touch. And it was enough to send Petra scooting back to her bedroom.

Where she fell face first onto her bed, her body thrumming as if she were wearing the wrong skin.

She glanced at her bedside drawer, where Russell was tucked up alseep, and whimpered at the knowledge that he was far too noisy to bring him out to play.

CHAPTER FOUR

THE NEXT MORNING Petra waited till she was in the lift before pulling on her ankle boots. She'd not dared risk the *chock-chock-chock* of her heels, or the loud *burr* of the espresso machine, in case she woke Sawyer.

As far as she could tell, he wasn't up yet. While the couch where she'd left him, all long and warm and gorgeous, had been tidied, as if the night before had never happened.

But what had happened? A movie night between mates with a quick platonic foot rub thrown in. Nothing at all!

Petra waved to the security guard behind the front desk, slid her big sunglasses onto her face and headed out into early morning grey.

To find a guy pointing his phone her way.

She shot him a quick smile, innate politeness kicking in, before she made to go down the hill, only he moved to step in her way. Which was when she noted the khakis and matching puffer jacket. It was the same guy from outside Sawyer's hotel. Meaning this was actually happening.

Instinct had her holding up her hand in front of

her face. Instinct *then* had her dropping it when she realised it only made her look like some poor man's Greta Garbo.

"You and Sawyer Mahoney?" he said, looking at her through the viewfinder. "You guys shacked up? What's your name?"

She'd had a little media experience, but the questions had been directed to the artists, had not been about *her*.

This was very different. She could feel his judgement. Feel his antagonism. As if this stranger had taken one look at her and decided she was lacking.

"Who do you think you are?" the guy asked, or maybe he'd just asked her name again.

Either way, her vision began to blur, her ears hummed, the way they had when she was a kid and her parents had paraded her before their friends and colleagues. Their gazes hard as they waited to see how she might fail them yet again.

The urge to spin back into the apartment building was a strong one. But she wasn't a kid any more. She wasn't failing anyone either. And she had to get to work.

Enough blood rushed back to her feet that she was able to remember some of Sawyer's instructions:

"Engage, but don't encourage...take the photo... control your own narrative..."

What was the narrative? They were friends who watched sultry French cinema together?

"Do all that and it's over sooner rather than later. Bring it to a close quickly."

That she could do—hopefully.

"Sorry!" she said in a sing-song voice, giving the guy a big smile and a friendly wave, even as her heart beat in her throat. Then she kept on walking. "Can't chat. Have to get to work! Have a great day!"

Heart racing, knees wobbling, she made it to the end of the block. Ducking around the corner, she glanced back to find he'd not followed. She pulled out her phone, sent Sawyer a text, letting him know what had happened.

Pretty sure he'd go all caveman if he thought she'd been in any real danger, she added that she was fine, his advice had worked, she'd handled it like a pro. Then wished *him* a great day, as clearly that had become her go-to sign-off.

Seriously. When she'd first agreed to come home she'd imagined herself sweeping in, magically whipping up a bunch of money, her parents gasping at how capable she truly was, then heading back in time to take up the offer to curate the art for a certain award-winning actress's new villa at Lake Como.

Instead she was tiptoeing out of her apartment so as not to wake her houseguest, and now hiding from paparazzi, or whoever that guy was. And she'd yet to raise a single cent.

She pushed herself away from the wall and

headed to the dry-cleaners, where she handed the woman her ticket stub. And checked her watch for her latest notifications, in case Sawyer had replied to her messages.

He had not.

"Sniff it."

Petra looked up to find the dry-cleaner holding up her garment bags, one of which had been zipped open, revealing the dusky pink tulle she'd worn on Saturday night.

Petra duly sniffed. "New detergent?"

The dry-cleaner shook her head and smiled proudly. "It took some doing, but we were able to save the dress *and* remove the heady scent of rum."

Petra opened her mouth to insist, once again, that she did not drink rum, when she heard club music thumping, saw rainbow lights swirling about her head, tasted tequila on the back of her tongue.

And from nowhere a memory from Saturday night unspooled in her mind…

"It's been so long, Sawyer," she said, twirling a hot pink feather she'd gathered up after it had fallen from one of the hen night girl's boa.

"Since?"

"Since I've let down my hair, you know?"

Sawyer watched her hand as she ran it over her hair, checking she had, in fact, let it down.

"It's busy business, being a wanted woman."
Petra tipped up onto her toes, her cheek all but

brushing against his as she shouted to be heard above the music. "It doesn't leave much time to swipe right, or date, or...or find myself backed up against a hard surface."

At that, Sawyer reared back, swallowing hard, his eyes dark.

Too squiffy to care, Petra said, "Then, and this is the real kicker, any time I do go on a date with some random, it feels like I'm cheating on Russell."

"Who the hell's Russell?" Sawyer asked. "I thought you just said you were too busy to...you know."

Petra wiggled her fingers over her ears, intimating Russell's particular shape. Then stage-whispered, "Russell's my favourite vibrator."

Sawyer swore. Rather a lot. Though with his hand rubbing over his beard it was kind of hard to tell.

"You?" Petra asked, realising she'd been talking about herself for quite a while.

"No favourite vibrator," he murmured.

Petra rolled her eyes and poked him in the chest, her finger bouncing off the hard flesh beneath. "Women," she said, placing her hand over his heart, or, to be precise, his left pectoral muscle, which was impressive as hell. "Flesh and blood. Soft skin and wicked moans."

Sawyer's chest lifted under her palm and she looked up at him to find his eyes on hers. Those clear blue eyes, now smoky and warm. Then his knee brushed against her. An electric shock shot through her. Enough that she gasped. But she did not move clear. And neither, she noticed, did he.

Some latent self-protection instinct that the tequila could not touch had her pulling her hand back to her side and saying, "I bet you have no such problems. Groupies galore beating down your door."

Sawyer breathed out hard, a mix of humour and exasperation now lighting the dark depths of his eyes.

His fingers tapped the space next to the half-empty tequila bottle as he said, "I've rarely spent more than a few nights in the same city, much less country, for months. Slept in tents, atop a Range Rover, in a treehouse just last week. Haven't had an actual shower with soap and hot water and a clean towel in some time. So I've hardly been in a position to..."

He stopped, with smoke still swirling in his eyes, his voice low and intimate, leading Petra to finish his sentence.

"Back a woman up against a hard surface?"

He laughed at that. Or choked. Again, she was finding it tricky to pick up on his signals. Darned tequila.

"Come on, Mahoney," she said, her voice feeling a little thick. "You must know that none of

that fancy stuff makes a lick of difference where you are concerned."

"Fancy stuff?" he said, his gaze warming. And had he moved in closer? It sure felt as if he had.

"The Sawyer Mahoney appeal goes beyond showers," she said loftily, her hand flying out sideways as if to emphasise her point.

Which was when it landed smack in the face of a passing drinks waiter.

A tumbler of rum, filled with ice, splashed over her dress—

"Here. Pocket stuff."

Petra blinked to find herself still at the dry-cleaners, several garment bags hooked over her elbow, the dry-cleaner handing her a small Ziplock bag containing what looked like a receipt, a hot pink feather and the pull tab from a soft drink can.

Head spinning, Petra popped the pocket stuff into her handbag, thanked the dry-cleaner and left, certain now that there was a *lot* she did not remember about that night with Sawyer.

Sawyer, who'd not been with anyone in goodness knew how long.

Sawyer, who was now staying in her apartment.

Sawyer, who knew she had a favourite vibrator. Named Russell.

Some random paparazzi wannabe was suddenly the least of her worries.

Giving up on the idea of walking to work, she held out her hand for a taxi, slipped her garment bags onto the back seat and gave the driver the gallery's address.

Feeling ninety-three percent sure that putting it all out of her head and simply pretending everything was hunky-dory was not only the right way to go, but possibly the most Gilpin thing she'd ever done.

Sawyer swung back and forth in the office chair he'd pulled up to Hadley's desk, checking the weather, the footy news, his messages, to see his little sister Daisy still hadn't responded.

Then he found a pencil and flipped it around his fingers. Till Hadley grabbed it from him and threw it across the room.

She said, "Go away."

"Give me something to do," he begged. "To fix. To disentangle. Give me a day trip. Anywhere."

"Not happening. You have things to do here. People to charm. So that we can afford to send you places. Now go away."

"I will," he said. "When the others get in."

"Ted is working from home today as his little one has a sniffle. Ronan took the jet to Perth overnight." She spared him a glare. "Can't you go for a run? Or lift something heavy, over and over again?"

"Did that already."

Awake with the birds, despite the late movie, and subsequent dreams of hands sliding over wet clay, over warm skin, he'd left the apartment stupid early that morning to sweat it out in the Big Think gym. Not that it had helped. Clearly.

His phone buzzed and he whipped it from his pocket. *Petra.*

Just seeing her name gave him an electrical charge. Only this time it came with the memory of her feet on his lap, her skin beneath his touch. Petra, whose eyes had turned dark, cheeks a warm telling pink when he hit the right spot. Petra, who knew how to pick a movie.

Then he read her message.

Hey, so there's a photographer outside the apartment. If you can call a goofy guy with an iPhone a photographer. He took some photos. Asked questions about us. I took your advice and played nice and then he left me alone. I'm fine, just letting you know so you can avoid him. Okay. Have a great day!

And every other thought dried up in a flash.

He'd left before her, left her alone, and this had happened. On his watch.

He typed back:

I'm on my way.

And then pushed back the seat so hard as he stood it smacked against the wall.

Hadley, used to working with the Big Think men, kept on typing. "Problem?"

"It's Petra. She had a photographer take photos of her outside our apartment this morning."

Her tapping came to a halt. "*Our* apartment?" Petra had typed back.

No need. I'm fine. Just wanted to give you the heads-up.

Hadley said, "I thought you'd taken the Big Think suite at the Elysium."

"I did. Now I'm staying at hers." Sawyer's thumbs hovered over his phone as he figured out…how to convince her she needed him. Yep, that was his thought process. Which was nuts. If she said she was fine, then she was fine.

"Sawyer—"

"Not now, Hadley."

"Yes now! It might seem ridiculous to you, but *I* need to know these things. You go rogue for months, playing hero on your metaphorical white steed, while Ted goes from saving the world to changing nappies, and Ronan is pissing off as many investors as he brings in due to his innate lack of humility. I'm the one holding this place together with my bare hands. So if you plan to add to my workload by taking part in some clickbait romantic entanglement that takes focus off the Big Think Ball—"

Sawyer held out a hand. "Petra is an old friend. We haven't seen one another in years. I'm staying in her spare room so we can catch up. That's all."

All true, and yet he felt his eye twitch.

Hadley raised her eyebrows. "So long as you know what you're doing."

Sawyer did not, as it turned out, know what he was doing. He just knew he had to do something. "I have to go."

"Best news I've had all day!" Hadley called as he left her office.

Adrenaline too high, he took the stairs.

Not because he liked playing hero, as Hadley asserted. But someone had to stand up, do the hard thing, do the right thing, and as usual that someone would be him.

Outside the Big Think skyscraper the sky was a murky grey. No rain, but no sun either, giving the architecture a kind of gloomy elegance. It was Melbourne at its most Melbourne.

Sawyer scanned the area and spied no paps, meaning this guy—whoever he was—wasn't interested in where he worked, only where he slept. Not great.

He turned the collar of his leather jacket up against the cool and set off, hustling past designer shops and stately hotels, past theatres and alleyways and converted churches. Past fences covered in posters for bands stuck up over older posters for bands. And walls covered in graffiti that reminded him of his sister, Daisy.

Needing something to settle his mind, he pulled his battered phone from his pocket and tried calling his youngest sister again, not expecting her to answer. But she did. And his relief was palpable.

"Hey, brother," said Daisy.

"Who is this?" he said.

A beat, then, "You called me, you doofus."

"You Called Me, You Doofus…? Hmm. Not ringing any bells."

Daisy groaned, while Sawyer checked both ways before jogging across the street.

"Where the heck have you been, kiddo?" he relented. "I've been trying to get onto you for days, to let you know that I'm in town so that you might rejoice."

"I've been about. Doing my thing."

Her thing being skateboarding and 'street art' which had led to him having to quietly get her out of trouble more times than their mother would ever know.

"Want to do me a solid and find a moment in between *things* to call Mum? Story around town, she's been lovingly requesting a check-in for a few weeks now."

"Hounding, more like."

Sawyer ran a hand over his mouth, not liking

the tone in her voice. His other sisters were uncomplicated, high-spirited creatures prone to creating babies, which was keeping his mother blissfully happy for the first time in his living memory.

Then there was Daisy. Solemn, shy, prone to depression. A lot like their mum used to be. Which was why his mum worried. And called. A guy could only try to save the world for so long before family responsibility wanted its turn.

"You think that's hounding?" he said. "Try this. Tell me where you are. Right now. Do it, do it, do it."

She laughed, as he'd hoped she would. "Yeah, maybe."

He rounded a corner and the spires on the Gallery of Melbourne popped into sight. "How are you? Really?"

A slow exhalation of breath. Then, "I am good. I'm actually starting to make a name for myself with my work, which is really cool. Mum just doesn't understand it."

He opened his mouth to say he didn't much understand it either, but the trundle of trams making a racket as they rocketed past gave him just enough pause to hear the words in his head. Which were embarrassingly similar to what Petra had heard daily as a kid. And he'd seen how divisive that lack of understanding could be.

Josiah and Josephine Gilpin were smart people. Yet they'd never been able to see how impressive their daughter was, and had always been, in her own unique way.

"Sawyer?"

"Yep. I'm here. And I'm chuffed for you, kiddo," he said, stopping to let a dogwalker with ten yappy dogs in a myriad of fancy collars make their way around him. He looked down to find a small pink gem, likely from the collar of one of the dogs. He picked it up and slipped it into his pocket. "Still, if you need me, need anything—"

Daisy sighed gustily. "I know the others live for your knight-in-shining-armour thing, but I don't need all that, okay?"

Sawyer reared back. What was it with the women in his life and their sudden need to psychoanalyse him?

A guy walking the other way glared at him, so he took a step sideways and set off on his mission once more. For it was who he was and they could all just handle it.

"Fine," Sawyer said, not meaning it. He'd turn himself up to annoyingly painful older brother level soon, but the gallery was in sight and he set off at a jog. "I'll be in touch again soon."

"I have no doubt," Daisy said, before hanging up.

When Sawyer barrelled into the gallery, a security guard looked up, and smiled. A few old ladies on a day out checke d their bags and umbrellas.

A toddler ran past his legs, a beleaguered-looking mother chasing.

It was all so pedestrian, it hit him – was he looking for problems to fix just to keep himself busy?

No. Unlike his family's loss, or Finn's accident, or the people he helped all over the world, Petra's current problem was all because of him.

He found signs pointing the way to admin.

When he found Petra in the back office area, she was sitting behind a desk in a glass-walled office at the far end of the space. Her small form was swamped by her oversized mustard-coloured jumper, beneath the desk dark fitted jeans were rolled at the cuff, over chunky ankle boots, showing off a sliver of pale skin in between.

And the memory of holding those ankles in his hands hit him like a truck. The warmth of her skin, the softness. How good it had felt. How right.

He leaned against the doorjamb and watched her rock side to side on her office chair, tapping a pencil against her teeth while she read something on her phone that was making her smile. Music played via a portable speaker set up on the corner of her messy desk. Surrounded by noise and light and a little mess, so sure of herself, in her element, it was clear she was not in need of someone to ride up and rescue her. Not in need of him.

And that hit harder than a truck ever could.

Then she looked up, saw him and cried, "Sawyer!", nearly dropping her phone, the pencil clattering from her hand, having to reach for it to stop it rolling off the table.

"Petra," he said, easing into the room as if he weren't in the midst of an existential crisis.

"Please tell me you're not here because of what happened," she said, pressing her chair back and standing. "I told you, I'm fine."

He rolled a shoulder. "I can see that. It's just—"

A shadow moved in beside him. It belonged to a pocket-sized brunette with a tablet in hand. Like a mini-Hadley in the making.

"Petra," she said breathlessly, "Murray Landis just emailed. He's in. Everything you asked for is yours."

"Yes!" Petra clapped her hands and bounced up and down, joy radiating from her.

The young woman at Sawyer's side grinned at Petra, then looked at Sawyer and said, "Oh! Sorry, I didn't see you there. It's… Oh, my, it's you!"

"It's me."

"Sawyer," said Petra, "this is Mimi Lashay, my wondrous sidekick in this endeavour. Mimi, Sawyer Mahoney."

Mimi juggled her tablet and held out a hand. "Big fan. Big. Huge. So good to meet you."

Sawyer smiled and shook. "Likewise."

The young woman looked from Sawyer to

Petra and back again. Then she left, muttering about wanting to be Petra when she grew up.

Petra hustled Sawyer into the room and shut the door. Pointed at the couch. "Sit."

Sawyer sat, waiting for Petra to sit at the other end. But after a moment's hesitation she leant her backside against her desk instead. He wondered if she was thinking about the night before too.

"Murray Landis?" he said, knowing a little about the up-and-coming tech guru.

"A new donor. We put out a lot of feelers yesterday, Mimi and I. Throwing spaghetti at the wall hoping something might stick. A few have shown slight interest, Murray the biggest so far. A tech trader looking for some good PR and to invest in his private collection. I offered advice as a sweetener."

"You're not mucking about, are you?"

"Right." Petra smiled, radiating confidence. Which was new. No, not new, just more overt than it had once been. She'd grown into her gravitas. "Which is good news, because while I keep getting these big fun ideas as to how this place could really be turned around, it's not in my purview. The sooner I raise the funds the sooner I can get back to my life."

"I thought you said you had the apartment for six months," he said, a strange tightness in his chest.

She blinked. "I do. Just in case. But my hope

was to blitz this gig then head back to London as soon as humanly possible."

Emphasis on the *was*. As if that hope had since changed.

"So," she said, looking away, "as you might have gathered, Mimi is a big fan."

"Huge," Sawyer corrected. "Which is nice, but can we talk about the elephant in the room?"

"Elephant?"

"The photographer."

"Oh, right." She nibbled at a thumbnail and he knew he'd made the right decision, coming to her.

"Was he polite? Did he touch you? Threaten you?"

"No! None of that. It all happened so fast." She shrugged. "Do you think it will keep happening?"

He sat forward, resting his elbows on his knees. He didn't want to worry her but also wanted to give her enough so that she could make an informed choice.

"In my footy days I couldn't have coffee without being tagged in a hundred pictures. People were usually pretty nice, unless they went for another team. But even then—"

"You were beloved," she said.

He couldn't help but laugh. "I was lucky. These days, I'm relatively boring as far as the paps are concerned. Out of sight, out of mind."

"Till now."

Sawyer nodded. "In the end it comes down to access. Without pictures there is no story."

"And with them…they can make up any story they like?"

Sawyer held out his hands, face up, in agreement. Then opened his mouth to offer help, but she held up a hand, halting him, while she had some thoughts.

The urge to take over, to fix everything, was not a surprise. The tightness in his chest as he waited to see what she chose to do was.

Petra looked through the glass wall and said, "I reckon I can handle it. It was a surprise, which was why it caught me off-guard. But I'm tougher than I look. Inured to judgement!"

Only because, as a kid, she'd had to be. Which made this kind of thing much harder. For her and for him.

"My one concern," she said. "Just quietly, the last guy who was in my position left under a cloud. I'd hate for any story to mess with what we are trying to do here."

Ready with a ten-point plan, including carrying her off to the nearest tower and locking her up inside, Sawyer heard Hadley's words, and Daisy's, and instead found himself asking, "Tell me what *you* need? Would you like me to move back to the hotel?"

"No!" she said, eyes flashing. "Don't even think about it. I've missed you, Sawyer. I didn't realise how much till I saw you the other night. I'm not about to let some stranger get in the way of us spending whatever time together we can. Okay?"

The violence of her response yanked at something inside him. Some thread that had been living, latent inside him, just waiting for her to tug. Now tugged, the floodgates opened and all kinds of feelings flew about inside him.

"Screw 'em," she said.

"Screw 'em," he agreed, his voice ragged.

And Sawyer felt, no, he *knew*, that they were in this thing together. Which, for the guy who usually shouldered the load single-handed, was a hell of a thing.

Then she had to go and shift against the desk, all slinky and loose. Her gaze locked on his in a way that made the feelings rushing through him spark and twist.

"At this point," she said, "I think I need to know what happened the other night. If anything happened. Forewarned is forearmed and all that."

"Like?"

"A few things have come back. The rum—a spill down my dress. And…" Eyes half closed, she lifted her hands to the top of her head and waggled her fingers.

Russell, the vibrator.

Hearing her wax lyrical about her favourite vibrator while two sheets to the wind was one thing, but sitting in her office, her standing there looking all warm and lovely and making him feel as if he was sitting by the fire on a cold day, was like heaven and hell all at once.

"That was educational," he drawled.

She lifted her hands to her face, her voice muffled as she said, "That has to be the worst of it, right?"

"You're a happy drunk. Chatty. Friendly. But there was no tabletop dancing, or bra-tossing, or fistfights, if that's your concern."

"It kind of was." Then she let her hands drop, crossing her arms, crossing her ankles. Those damn ankles. And she asked, "And us…? There's no particular reason we are suddenly of interest to the press?"

"Such as?" he asked, his voice rough.

Thinking of how she'd found any chance to touch his arm, or smack him on the chest, or pluck fluff from his hair.

Thinking of how he'd felt as if he could have stayed there, talking to her, for the rest of his life. And how if it had been any other girl he'd have been entirely within his rights to believe they'd both been flirting their hearts out.

But this wasn't any other girl. This was Petra.

Her glance was deadpan. "Do you want me to list possibilities and you nod any time I'm right?"

No, he did not. "We talked, we laughed, we told stories. We reminisced."

"And that's all?"

Sawyer nodded. *Pretty much.*

"Great," she said with a huge sigh of relief.

Sawyer found himself glad she hadn't asked for a blow-by-blow account. For while there had been nothing the press would find interesting, not while they'd been at the main bar, there had been moments he'd be hard pressed to explain. He could barely make sense of them himself, and figured they were best left to fading memory.

"Still, after this morning's fun, I'd like to pick you up and take you home tonight."

She blanked him. "Because the more they see the two of us together, the more likely they are to back off?"

Sawyer's jaw worked. She had him there.

"I'll be fine. I have the Sawyer Mahoney Rules of Engagement in my head. And a neat right hook." She shifted back and forth, fists raised in such a way she'd break her thumb if she made contact at all. "Now, leave. I have to get back to work."

Making it clear, there was no knight in shining armour position for him as far as she was concerned.

And when she lifted her chin, daring him to contradict her, out of nowhere he was reminded of Finn. And it was like a bucket of ice water poured over his head.

If Finn had still been around, watching them

circle one another the way they had been, would he have warned him off? Or would he have laughed it off as inevitable?

It was something Sawyer would never know.

He pulled himself to standing. "Is it okay with you if I try to get Daisy over for dinner one night?"

"Of course! Did you get onto her?"

"I did."

"Oh, that's fabulous! I still picture her in pigtails, all ringlets and red bows. How is she?"

"No longer wearing pigtails. And painting Melbourne in graffiti."

Petra burst into laughter, before it came to a sudden stop. "Oh, you mean literally. Wow. Is she any good?"

"At tagging fences near train lines?" He had no clue. "What's the criteria?"

"Does she have a site? Socials?"

He nodded.

"Show me."

"Her eyebrow rings?"

"Her work."

Sawyer found his sister's Instagram page and handed over his phone. Moving to lean his backside against the desk beside her, he watched as she scrolled and scrolled, gaze intent on the screen, her profile a study in delicate architecture.

"How have I not seen this before now?" she asked, turning to face him, their faces danger close. Her eyes now filled with fire and determination. "What does she eat? Any intolerances or predilections?"

"I can cook."

She shook her head. "I know a great place round the corner. I'll order in."

"I. Can. Cook."

She blinked at him, big eyes, tangled lashes, a constellation of pale freckles scattering the bridge of her nose. "How?"

"The usual way. Ingredients, heat."

She swallowed; her pupils dilating. And he *knew* it had nothing to do with talk of food. "I wouldn't know," she said, handing him back his phone.

His thumb brushed hers as he took it back. Deliberately? Hell, yeah.

When he felt her gravity pulling him in, he stood. Then reached into his pocket, found the pink gem, waited for her to hold out her hand and dropped it into her palm. "Found it on my walk here. Thought of you."

"Oh," she said, her face lighting up with delight.

Figuring it best to quit while he was ahead, Sawyer moved to the door and said, "I'll leave you to it then."

Knocking the doorframe in goodbye, he left. If he whistled as he walked back towards the lift, not caring who was watching him, then so be it.

CHAPTER FIVE

"HURRY UP!" Petra called. "I can't believe you take longer to get ready than I do!"

After a few days of successfully avoiding men in khaki and puffer jackets, that Sunday morning Petra sat at the small round dining table, one leg crossed over the other, flicking lint off her leopard print skirt and olive-green polo neck.

"You don't look ready."

Petra looked up to find Sawyer standing near the kitchen, his hair a little damp from his shower, wearing dark jeans that did great things to all the bits they enclosed and a navy Henley, the crease marks from the packaging down his chest.

"Have you been shopping?" she asked, when what she wanted to say was *Phwoar!*

He glanced down and tugged at his shirt till half a pec peeked over the top of the neckline. And she came mighty close to having an aneurysm right there on the spot.

"I have a person who sends me clothes when I need them."

"A *stylist*?" she asked, loving the pink creeping over the top of his beard.

He let his shirt go and narrowed his eyes her way. If he realised she was babbling to cover her lust, then he didn't say so. Except his eyes did glint just a little before he asked, "You okay?"

"Yep!" she said, snapping out of her fog and shooting to her feet.

"Because you look a little flushed."

"Nope. Trick of the light. Now, let's go bother your sister!"

They were on their way to see Daisy. Unable to lock her down to a dinner—*too bourgeoise*—she'd agreed to a catch-up when she'd heard Petra was coming. Which Sawyer had taken in his stride.

The truth was, after days of making very few inroads into scraping up donations, Petra finally had the seed of a plan. A plan that could see the gallery not only get itself out of its current financial straits, but to become a true destination for art enthusiasts, in a city that prided itself on being the cultural hub of Australia.

As fun as Deena was, she fitted into the Gilpins' world, not Petra's. The contacts Deena had would likely look at Petra as if she had two heads. Whereas Daisy? Now *she* might be the key.

Petra grabbed the gift she'd picked up for Daisy on her way out of the door. Sawyer held it open, forcing Petra to pass him nice and close. The scent of his skin, freshly washed, the size of him swamping her made her feel all buoyant. And woozy.

She let out a great big sigh. Then looked up to find him smiling, as if he knew exactly why. And while it ought to have her in a panic, the truth was, the more time they spent together, making new memories, ones that were wholly their own, the more she found herself hoping he'd hurry up and figure it out.

"Oh, shut up," she said, heading to the lift with the sound of his laughter in her ears.

In the lift, and out, Petra walked backwards towards the rear doors, grateful the building manager had given them permission to use the emergency exits any time they left the building. "Cab? Walk? Tram?"

"Wait—" said Sawyer, his expression suddenly grim as he held out a hand, but Petra was through the doors before she saw the crowd gathered in the back alleyway.

Camera flashes snapped and mobile cameras hovered in front of her face.

"What the hell?" she said, rearing back. Hitting smack bang into a wall.

I can handle it, she quickly reminded herself. *I'm tougher than I look. I'm inured to judgement!*

And yet she froze. The same way she had when her parents' colleagues barked questions at her. Questions Finn had answered as if born with them lined up inside his head. While she'd just wanted to hide under a table and trace the wood patterns she found there.

Then the wall at her back moved. It was Sawyer stepping in beside her and taking her by the hand.

"I've got you," he said, his words brushing over her ear as he smiled into the distance. Then, his voice warm, charming, strong and sure, cutting through the throng, he said, "Excuse us, guys. My friend and I are running late."

Questions came at them, too fast, too convoluted for Petra to pick out a single thread. The blood rushing behind to her ears didn't help. Or the fact her feet had gone numb, as if all the blood had left her body. She hated it. Hated that it made her react this way.

Sawyer's voice, her lifeline in the stormy sea, said, "Petra, sweetheart, we need to go." Then he slipped an arm around her waist and used it to herd her forwards.

And she stuck by him, like glue. Her body pressed against his. And before she knew it, they were in a taxi, Sawyer giving her a small push across to the far end of the back seat so he could climb in after her.

She heard him bark an address, and they were off.

Her hearing came back fully after a minute or so, to find Katie Melua singing through the tinny speakers. And she turned to face Sawyer, who was watching her, his whole body tensed, as if readying to strike anyone who dared disagree with her, much less jump out and take her photo.

"Taxi, then?" she asked.

And after a beat Sawyer burst out laughing. Then, as if that had magically broken the body-guard spell that had come over him, he ran his hands over his face and swore, an impressive array of language choices all focused at the mob.

Energy flowing around him like a summer wild aura, he said, "It's been niggling at me, how this has all gone down. And I think I've figured it out. The guy, the one who took your photo the other day, khakis and puffer jacket? He was there. Only he's not a pap. He's just some guy who was at the bar the other night. He asked for my auto-graph, but I was heading to the bathroom so made an excuse and brushed him off. I'd totally forgot-ten about it till I saw him just now."

He breathed out hard. "I'd put money on him being a fan, with zero intention of selling any photo he took. Something changed that, clearly. And he made the rookie mistake of also giving up where we were."

"Who needs paparazzi when you have super-fans?" she said. "As for the rest of them, are we— as in me—really that interesting?"

Sawyer lifted a hand as if writing across the sky. "Handsome, Beloved, Footy Star Billionaire Philanthropist with a Heart of Gold Tempted into Secret Tryst with Little- Known Society Prin-cess." A small sorry smile lifted his mouth as he said, "The headline writes itself."

Petra groaned. Then leant forwards and let her head fall into her hands.

She was going to have to call her mother, let her know that there might be…something. Not a *whiff of scandal* by any measure, but in her mother's eyes anything that wasn't neat, tidy, proper was disquieting.

Petra herself included.

Adrenaline levels having dropped, the backs of Petra's eyes burned. She bit her lip and forced herself to keep it together.

"Do not ask if I'm okay," she demanded when she heard Sawyer's intake of breath.

"I was about to assure you the *heart of gold* bit would *never* happen."

At that she laughed. Then groaned again.

"Are you okay?"

"Stop! Seriously. You need to stop asking me that! It is doing my head in!" She glanced over to see a muscle twitch beneath his eye.

Other than that, he seemed wholly unfazed by her outburst, as if his reasons trumped hers. "It eases my mind."

"I'm aware. I am. And I get why."

He stilled. Braced. But it was time he faced up to this. Truly. Now seemed a good time, considering the only way he could avoid it was to leap from a moving car.

For he had it in him to run, if she pushed too

hard, too fast. He'd done it before. Twice. Just left, with no word, for a long time.

After Finn's funeral. And after her eighteenth birthday party.

A memory flickered—something to do with her eighteenth. But not the party itself, something from the night at the Gilded Cage. A conversation? Reminiscence? Re-enactment? She tried to reach out for it, but it fluttered just out of reach.+

"You feel the need to look out for me, because of Finn," she said.

His jaw clenched.

"It hurts you when I say his name, doesn't it?' she whispered. 'I'm sorry that it feels that way. Especially because I love telling stories about him. It gives me such solace. I won't force you, it's not my place. But I'm here, ready and willing, when you are. Till then, I need you to know that I would tell Finn the exact same thing, if he were still here: I've been looking after myself for a really long time now. And I've done a pretty good job of it. So take it as a given, unless I tell you otherwise, I'm just fine."

He said nothing, and she could only hope it had sunk in.

As for her, she'd not loved having to push through the mob, but she'd hated more the fact that she'd frozen. As if all the work she'd done to know herself, and love herself, even if her parents could not, was for naught.

She was not going to let that happen again. "Teach me your ways."

"Regards?" he asked, his jaw still tight.

"Connect Four," she shot back. Then gave his leg a nudge. And kept her knee there, near his, annoying him till he looked her way. "If you didn't notice, I just asked you for help. Which should have you on cloud nine. So can you get over yourself for a second, and help me?"

He looked at her then, his clear blue eyes taking her in. Then he glanced at her hand, resting by his thigh.

She wriggled her fingers, warning him she'd squeeze again if he didn't comply. "Teach me how not to freeze up."

He took a deep breath in, let it go, then said, "After my dad died, my mum had it hard—alone, young, four kids to raise. So she leaned on me." Then, "Stop me if I've told you this story."

Petra shook her head. "Go on."

"I'd been a bit of a handful, a class clown. But I had to stop making waves so my sisters could slide through on my wake. I taught myself how to cook. Did assignments on my lap while waiting for my sister to finish her after-school job, or with Daisy at the skate park.

"Then Daisy started to run away, all the time— from shops, from school. My heart would be in my throat the whole time, imagining all the terrible things that might have happened to her. But

I'd not let Mum see. Because how much harder would it have been for my mum if she knew how hard it was on me?"

Smile, she thought, *take the photo and thank them. As if it's your idea.*

He made it look so easy. When it wasn't. Not at all.

Oh, Sawyer.

"You became good at pretending," she said.

He nodded. "Looking back," he said, "those years are a total blur. Till—" A quick frown marred his forehead.

"Till?" she encouraged. Knowing in her gut what was coming next, and hoping, *hoping* this time he might be the one to bring it up.

"Till your brother ditched that fancy private school footy team and joined mine."

There, she thought, an overwhelming sense of gratitude coming over her. If that craziness outside the apartment building had led to this, then she'd take it.

"He was quite the light-bringer, that brother of mine," she said.

Sawyer let his head fall back against the seat. "Yeah. He was all right, I guess. But your house— spotless, quiet, food prepped by a cook. Now that was bliss."

Petra shivered. "Your reprieve was my nightmare."

Sawyer laughed, the sound rough. Then he

opened his eyes and tipped his head to face her. That face, those eyes, that soul. She let out a sigh before she'd even felt it coming.

His gaze dropped to her mouth, and her instincts began to hum.

"Now it all makes sense," he said, dragging his gaze back to hers. "The shoes you discard at the door, the jacket tossed over the back of the couch, the constant music playing or the balcony door open to let in the noise of the city. You're still rebelling."

She laughed. "A little bit."

He smiled. She smiled. And when his chest rose and fell, she wondered if maybe there was even the slightest possibility that he wasn't completely immune to her too.

Then his hand found hers, curling around her fingers, before he lifted it onto his leg, where he traced the lines on her palm and she literally forgot how to breathe.

"Do you remember the day we met?" she asked, then cleared her throat to dislodge the bur within.

"I remember feeling terrified I'd get footy mud on the clean floor. Till you walked in, sticks in your hair, a pink flower tucked into the knot of your overalls, trailing grass up the hall. It was like spotting a unicorn in the wild. And I knew that I'd never have to pretend for you."

Petra swallowed as the sweetness of his words climbed under her skin, curled up and purred.

Then the taxi stopped suddenly, the tyres screeching for a half second. The driver looked over his shoulder, saying, "Sorry, guys. Learner driver just pulled out in front."

"All good, mate," Sawyer said, instant charm.

Then, with one last swipe of his thumb down her palm, he gave Petra back her hand. She curled it into her lap, her nerves singing, her instincts dancing in circles.

"So what happens now?" Petra asked.

"We visit Daisy."

She'd meant with the photographers. "But—"

"We visit Daisy. You guys chat art. Then we get on with our day. You can't let it sit with you. Or worry you. You can only control what you can control, which is you. Your behaviour, your response. Which for me means acting as if I'm not enraged by a bunch of strangers camped out in the alley behind my unicorn friend's building, taking photos and yelling at her, because that would only give the story legs. And because she wants to learn to handle it herself."

Petra reached out and took his hand, holding it between them.

And they stayed that way for the final couple of blocks' drive down the street to meet his sister.

"Here will do," Sawyer told the taxi driver, peeling off some cash so they could hop out fast, just in case.

But no one had followed. They were interesting on a slow news day, but they were not royalty. Meaning the day was hers. And she was going to make the most of it.

"This way," said Sawyer, shooting her a smile as he held out a hand.

And she took it, because apparently that was now a thing that they did. Yep, the day was looking up already.

He led her down a tall, dark, narrow alleyway and Petra was instantly transported. For on both sides of the alleyway, every inch of reachable wall space was covered in colour. Some dull, some recent. Some paint. Some chalk. Including a glorious mural of Frida Kahlo—untouched by the graffiti tags covering every other wall.

"Honour among thieves," said Sawyer, who'd stopped beside her, hands in pockets, admiring the artistry.

Then he pointed to a bright white painting of a daisy in the middle of a mural filled with quotes over the top of quotes till it was too hard to pick out where one started and another began.

Petra stood back and took it in, her heart now beating hard in her chest, a feeling she'd not had since coming home, no matter how many triptychs she had leaning against the hallway wall, or light installations she'd installed. To know that her inspiration could spark here was a huge relief. "Wow. This is…"

"A cry for help?" said Sawyer.

"Glorious," Petra chastised, before noting that he was smiling, his eyes filled with wonder as he looked over what was clearly his sister's work.

"I jest. But the first time she was caught," he said, "the owner of the building called the police. Daisy was arrested. Mum rang, panicked. The entire family was up in arms. I, of course, was called on to sort it out."

"How?" Petra asked, spotting a piece of pink chalk and picking it up.

"I bought the building."

Of course he did.

"Best big brother ever," she said, then realised what she'd said. An unexpected flash of sorrow poured through her, in the place she usually saved for nothing but lovely memories. "I mean, not *the* best, but—"

"I know," he said, taking her hand and tucking it into his elbow. "And I am happy to share the title with Finn."

"Petra!"

Petra turned to find Daisy barrelling towards them. Short dark hair dipped in hot pink. Studs in her ears and on her clothes. Black lipstick. The same bright blue eyes as her big brother.

Petra gathered Daisy in for a hug, then pointed to Daisy's work. "I'm blown away. Truly."

"You love it," she said, with a measure of pride that Petra adored.

Sawyer moved in to give his sister a big bear hug, which she took. And again Petra found herself awash with bittersweet feelings.

"I love it too," Sawyer assured his sister.

"Sure you do," said Daisy, pulling back to roll her eyes at her brother.

"Sprung." Petra laughed. "Art is subjective, and that's a good thing. If we all loved the same painting, there would only be one painting. And then where would you be?"

Daisy took that in, and nodded at her wall. "I like that. Can I quote you?"

"I'd be honoured. Also…" Petra reached into her oversized bag and pulled out the sculpture she'd found a couple of days before on one of her lunchtime jaunts. "A present."

"Is this a Tabitha Mendez?" Daisy asked, her voice overawed as she took in the sharp angles and bright colour.

Petra nodded. "I saw it and thought of you."

"I can't. That's way too much."

Petra held up both hands. "My dream in life is to bring art to the person who'll love it the most. Do you love it?"

"I love it."

"Then it's meant to be. Now, I know you're busy—"

Daisy wasn't, but she puffed up at the thought Petra assumed she was.

"So I'll get right to the point. I'm working with

the Gallery of Melbourne, and playing with an idea that would bring a whole lot of freshness to the place. I was hoping you could be my conduit. Show me what's new in town. Introduce me to some of your artist friends."

Daisy blinked, still slightly stunned by the gift, which Petra had fully expected she might be. "Sure. But they are hardly Gallery of Melbourne types."

"I get that. But that's what excites me about them. This idea, it's more of an…epic dream, if you will Drinks on me one night, so I can pick your brains?"

"That'll do it," Daisy said with a grin.

Petra glanced to where Sawyer was standing back, a smile on his face, his eyes on her. Eyes filled with warmth. And something else. Some slice of himself Petra knew was all for her.

She could feel the heat of it, a knife-edge, hot and focused, like the run of his thumb down her palm, the brush of his breath over her ear when he'd called her *sweetheart* before ushering her to the taxi.

Then she remembered he'd *just* told her a story about how good he was at pretending. That he'd spent his life fitting himself into whatever mould he needed to be. Perfect son. Protective brother. Football star. Social justice warrior. Billionaire philanthropist. Friend.

Not with her, he'd assured her. He'd not had to

pretend back then. But now? With so many more ghosts now heavy on his shoulders?

"Your brother looks hungry," Petra said, pushing her toes into her shoes when his eyes flared with a different kind of hunger.

She turned back to Daisy. "Come with me while I feed him?"

Aware that it was a ruse for her big brother to look after her by proxy, Daisy waited a beat before heading up the alleyway. "Go ahead and hold hands again, if you like. I don't mind."

"What?" said Petra. "That was… It wasn't…"

But Sawyer shot her a grin that had her mouth drying up. Then he had his sister in a headlock as the two Mahoneys strutted up the alleyway.

Leaving Petra with no choice but to follow.

I will not search for my name online. Or Sawyer's name. I will be calm and Zen and focused on the things that I can control.

That evening, after having messaged her mother to let her know that she and Sawyer might be in some photos, doing nothing but leaving her apartment building, and not to worry, she had it under control, Petra set her watch to Do Not Disturb.

Then she sat on the floor of the lounge room, TV playing a home renovation show on low volume, couch at her back, papers and highlighters and sketchpad at the ready. A glass bowl holding the gem, feather and piece of chalk sat before her like a talisman—a reminder that simple things could be the most beautiful. As she collated the zillion ideas she'd had since breakfast with Daisy.

Ears attuned, having lived with him for a few days now, she heard Sawyer's footsteps coming down the hall.

Like a moth to a flame she turned to find he was shirtless, his chest bare, showing off so many tattoos her poor eyes had no chance of absorbing them all.

Then there was the V-shaped muscle working its way from his abs to his…below ab area, loose pyjama bottoms hanging low off his hips.

And as he scrubbed his hair dry with a towel, the veins roping down his forearms were very much deserving of their own toast. And a statue. And maybe a public holiday.

Then, when he dropped the towel, she saw that he'd shaved.

And it was all she could do not to expire on the spot.

Rough and scruffy, he was a big, beautiful bear of a man. But like this…hair slicked back, hard jaw clean-shaven, that sensual mouth no longer hidden… She felt as if she had fallen into a deep hypnosis.

"Whoa," she said, the word falling from her open mouth before she could catch it.

Finding her in the semi-darkness—for night had fallen while she'd been busy working—his face broke into a grin, lines bracketing his mouth, the flash of a canine or two.

He lifted his hand to his jaw and gave it a rub.

"It's been itching like hell for days," he said. "I kept it in the hope it might give me a little anonymity, but that horse has clearly bolted. Still going?"

It took Petra a moment to figure out what he meant. She turned back to her papers. "I am. But it's good. Really good. And much more up my alley than calling people asking for money. Art is a connector. It's a conversation. It's collusion and community and colour and cool. Making the gallery the home for *that* kind of experience will bring in the money, I know it."

The couch behind her back shifted as Sawyer sat at the other end, bare foot beside her hip. The man half-naked, and damp and warm and smelling so good.

Feeling itchy, and twitchy, she twirled her hair into a bun atop her head. Only for it to fall loose within a minute.

"Can I put on the pre-game instead?" he asked, nodding towards the TV.

"Mm-hmm," she said, not trusting her voice.

He moved closer to reach past her to grab the remote from the coffee table, the heat of his skin washing over her. "I can watch it in silence if it'll disturb you."

"Sound up," she said, "white noise always best."

She gathered her hair and twirled it tighter this

time, needing as much air around her as possible. But it wasn't to be.

"Let me help." Sawyer, lifting his foot, scooted in behind her, trapping her between his knees. Then he gathered her hair in his hands.

"What's happening now?" she asked, pulling her head away, spinning on her butt, hands lifted as if she might fight him off.

"I'm helping."

"I thought you meant with work."

"What do I know about art?"

"What do you know about hair?"

"Three sisters," he reminded her, his clear blue eyes sparking, his mouth lifted at one corner, un-impeded by the beard, and *whoa*...

She knew she should say no, but instead found herself turning back to face the TV. Then his hands were in her hair again, lifting it gently from her neck, running through the lengths, gently de-tangling as he went.

Then he gave her head a gentle shake, her brain rattling against her skull.

"Hey! What was that for?"

"Stop thinking so much. I can practically hear it from here."

Petra doubted it very much. Would he be sit-ting so close if he knew how aware she was of his thighs? His bare chest? How she was memo-rising every place he touched her?

Then he leaned past her to grab the remote

again and she glanced sideways, catching his beautiful profile, the curls brushing over his ears, the scent of his skin. And it took every bit of self-control not to lean in and drink him in.

He turned up the volume just a smidge more. Went to sit back and stopped when he saw her notebooks. The sketches she'd made.

"Is this about Daisy?" he asked.

"Mmm hmm."

He turned to face her, close enough she could see a small patch on one cheek where he'd shaved not quite close enough. Could taste his clean skin on the back of her tongue.

His nostrils flared and he looked back at her notes. "Have you told her any of this?"

"Not yet. I'd hate to get her hopes up if I can't pull it off. I need this approved by the gallery management, which will take some Sawyer-level charm."

"What is it, exactly?"

Petra wriggled forward on her backside, glad to have a little breathing space, then found a larger sketch she'd made of the forecourt. "I want to showcase a slew of young artists in some kind of wild, bright, loud, joyous, family-friendly, ticketed special collection out front of the gallery."

He nodded.

"If successful—which it will be, because this is my wheelhouse—it would lead to future pop-ups, a constant rotation, each of which could have their own corporate or community sponsor, which will keep the gallery relevant and making money going forward. And I want Daisy's work to be the centrepiece. Her flowers, her quotes. She's seriously talented. And innovative. And cool. And her work is so joyful people will love it. They'll love her."

He handed back her sketch and said, "You're good."

"I know."

"I mean the sketch. I can see exactly what you mean. You've got talent."

"A little. I am a woman of many skills," she said, then sat back, her shoulders sliding into the gap between Sawyer's thighs. And she motioned to her head.

Laughing, he settled back into place and gathered her hair once more.

Only this time his hands moved to her scalp, sparks racing over her skin like static. Uncomfortable and fantastic, all at once. Till she felt restless. And unsettled. And lit up with want.

She could just make out his reflection in the TV while the commentators talked stats and scores regarding the last time the two teams had met. She watched the flexing of the muscles in his arms, the dark shadows of his tattoos reaching over his meaty shoulders, the way he watched his fingers move through her hair.

His voice was low, quiet as he said, "A big part of why I came home when I did was because

Mum was worried Daisy was feeling a little low, which for Daisy can mean a lot low. Then you stepped up and made everything a thousand times better than I ever could."

"Oh, I doubt that."

He shook his head. "Your confidence and lack of fuss; it was a masterclass in caring for someone without overstepping."

Petra wasn't sure she'd ever been given a compliment that meant as much. Coming from Sawyer, her heart fluttered like a bird in a cage.

"She's amazing," Petra said. "Which is why I want to do this. But I'm glad I could help. This is where you say, *Thank you, Petra.*"

Sawyer's gaze dropped to hers in the reflection. His mouth quirked and he said, "Thank you, Petra."

Then his fingers moved over her skull, tracing her temple, then down her neck, dipping below the collar of the oversized shirt she'd thrown on that evening. And there was no hope of stopping the sound of utter pleasure escaping her throat.

Then he carefully separated three chunks of hair at her crown.

Petra's eyes opened wide. "Are you...*braiding* my hair?"

"Best way to keep hair out of your face, yes?"

"How on earth—?"

"The girls all went through a Katniss Everdeen obsession. Now, shush, or I'll have to start all over again."

They sat in silence, the football on the TV, Sawyer's fingers gliding across her scalp with a tenderness she'd not have expected from those big hands of his.

And she let herself imagine what it might be like if this was her actual life. Not a blip, not serendipity, but actually *being* with Sawyer. Talking about each other's work, their stresses, their delights. Not having to find excuses to touch one another.

Only to find that imagining it lasting for ever made her realise they were already living on borrowed time.

Then his fingers reached the bottom of her skull, the soft spot where her baby hairs tickled her neck, and a shiver rolled through her. If he noticed he didn't say anything. Though he did take his time finishing the final strands.

"All done," he said when he tucked the end into itself.

She turned slowly to face him, hands running over his work, the plaits a little bumpy and uneven. Which only made her love it all the more. "I'm seriously impressed."

He half smiled, his eyebrows raised. "This is the part where you say, *Thank you, Sawyer.*"

"Thank you, Sawyer."

Gratified, he sat back, his thighs still pressing lightly against her shoulders. And rather than getting back to work, Petra stayed right where she was.

The noise of the crowd on the TV grew as the Magpies, Sawyer's old team, Finn's favourite, ran out.

"Do you miss it?" she asked.

"Sometimes," he said, not having to ask what. "The training was a bitch. But the mate-ship, the clear intent, the finesse of the game itself. Nothing like it."

"I know it was your life's dream, the both of you, to play professionally, but I do wonder sometimes if Finn would have gone on with it, or if he'd have been swept up into law as our folks intended."

"Mmm…" Sawyer said in a way that made her turn. Her arm hooked up onto his knee. His legs splayed before her, his chest sculpted perfection.

"What does that 'mmm' mean, exactly?"

He ran a hand through his hair, the curls springing up in damp whirls. "It wasn't my dream, in point of fact."

"Excuse me?"

"It was Finn's. And my dad's. A story my mum told me before every footy season, tears in her eyes."

Petra twisted further, accidentally gathering the fabric of his thin pyjama pants till they cupped him in a way that took every fibre of her being not to look.

"Are you telling me," she said, "that you were

a first-round draft pick for the most successful football club in the country, and you were doing it for…your best friend, and your dad?"

"Do you hear me complaining?"

His gaze dropped from the TV and landed on her. With no hair to hide behind she felt raw. Exposed. But she couldn't let that stop her. Not when she felt so close to unlocking some part of him she'd not even known was there.

"No!" she said. "Not at all. It's just… What *was* your dream? Your passion? That one thing you always felt you were meant to do?"

"Not everyone has that, Petra. You were born lucky."

Born lucky? Not something she'd ever considered before.

"What about now? Your Big Think work; it's amazing, right?"

He breathed deep, thought hard and said, "When the pre-organised jobs are done and I can wander, talk to the locals, find out what they need and make it happen, that feels pretty good. More buckets to collect spring water? Done. Wood, nails, tools to repair fences to keep out predators? Done."

"That sounds amazing," she said, and meant it. "Can you do *more* of that?"

"It's hard to find those kinds of stretches of spare time. Though…"

"Though what?"

"The one time I did have the time was during the long months of rehab, after busting my leg. Meeting with those kids, the ones whose parents couldn't afford regular sessions, then hustling to find places for them to get access to the level of care the club had afforded me, begging for funds for a brand-new rehab facility in Darwin, that was seriously rewarding. With Big Think the big stuff has to happen first. Ted's innovations. Ronan's greasing of palms and circumnavigating bureaucratic red tape. Only then do I get to do my stuff."

"So you do love it?"

"Mostly."

"Sawyer!"

"Mostly is pretty damn good."

Petra shook her head. This was blowing her mind. To think that, after all Sawyer had achieved, it was all down to what? Duty? Ability? Skill? Rather than impulse and desire and happiness, which were the things that drove every decision she made?

"Name one thing, off the top of your head, that you want. With a kind of urgency you can feel in your gut. Right now!"

He breathed out hard, shifting on the seat, and she couldn't help herself, she glanced down. And she had her answer.

Me, she thought. *He wants me.*

But she couldn't say it. Could barely believe it.

Couldn't reconcile her daydreams of for ever with something *actually* happening between them. For it would change their dynamic, messy as it was, for ever.

So she slowly untwisted, let his pyjamas fall back into place and pretended nothing was happening. And said, "What about a hobby, then?"

At that he laughed, the muscles in his chest clenching in ways that had saliva pooling in her mouth.

"A hobby?" he repeated.

"Like…macramé. Or golf. Or…" *What hobbies did other people enjoy?* "Rolling cheese down a hill."

"Cheese rolling?"

"It's a thing. Right?"

"What are your hobbies?" he asked, leaning forward, elbows resting on his knees. Abs crunching, not a lick of spare skin. "Petra?"

Her eyes lifted to his. "Sorry, what?"

"Hobbies," he repeated, his voice low, intimate. "Outside of work? Do you knit? Bowl?" A pause, then, "Date?"

Petra opened her mouth to tell him her work was her hobby, her hobby her work. Who needed to knit, or bowl, or run their hands down a man's chest, or slide their hand up his thigh, or press their lips to his smooth hard cheek when their work was so very satisfying?

"This isn't about me," she said, her voice barely louder than a whisper.

His gaze hooked on hers. Then he reached out to capture a stray curl of hair he'd missed and tucked it behind her ear. "I'm starting to wonder if it is. About you."

And there his hand stayed, his fingers gently cradling her jaw, his thumb running along her cheekbone. His gaze hazy. His jaw tight.

While spot fires lit up all over Petra's body. Pockets of heat and hope and flashes of panic, as Sawyer Mahoney looked at her like...

Like he wanted to kiss her.

Petra swallowed. And Sawyer's gaze dropped to her throat. To her chest, rising and falling as she sucked in great gusts of air. Then lifted to her mouth.

His thumb moved down her cheek to slide over the corner of her lips. Then along the crease. Tugging at her bottom lip, so gently, but enough that her mouth opened, and stayed that way.

While she didn't move. Didn't even breathe, in case it broke whatever magic spell had come over them both.

Then the siren blared on the TV, the opening bounce of the game, and Sawyer shook his head. Literally. As if clearing away a brain fog.

His hand dropped away.

He dragged his gaze to the TV, his jaw hard,

his expression fierce. As if he was having a hell of an argument inside his own head.

Then he pushed himself up on his palms, the veins in his forearms bulging as he shot out of the chair.

"You're not going to watch the game?" she asked. When what she really meant was, *You're just leaving me here, now, filled with this longing?*

"Nah. Put your home reno show back on, if you like. I'm going to take your advice."

"What advice?"

"I'm going to go find some cheese to roll."

Completely flummoxed, Petra waited till he came out of his room again, having pulled on jeans and a jumper, heading towards the front door.

"It might take a while," she called out, "considering we're in the middle of the city!"

She could have sworn he muttered, "Here's hoping," before he called, "Don't wait up," and was out of the door.

Leaving Petra to stare at the TV, then her notes, and wonder what the heck had just happened.

CHAPTER SIX

AFTER A RESTLESS NIGHT, waking up every time she thought she heard the front door open, the urge to check Sawyer's bedroom before she left for work was so strong it hurt.

But in the end he was his own man, who could come and go as he pleased. It had nothing— *nothing* to do with her. Of that, she was eighty... eighty-five percent sure. And he'd said it himself—all she could control was her reaction, her behaviour.

Which was why she called an early morning meeting with the gallery management team, making it clear it was in their best interests they all attend.

Dressed to impress in a forest-green belted silk dress, and her lucky aubergine boots, sparkly clips in her hair, she watched the faces of the gallery management team—most of whom had worked there since she was a kid, and all of whom looked more than a little overwhelmed by the Epic Dream Festival idea she'd just presented to them.

But she *knew* what she was doing. This—bringing art to people who needed it—was her happy place. *Her dream*. Where the years spent wandering, collecting seemingly disparate things, had purpose.

The rest of her life, not so much. Clearly, if a conversation about hobbies and knitting and rolling cheese could send a guy running for his life.

She shook herself back into the meeting. Leant forward and looked each person dead in the eye. "Pulling together this kind of event, from idea to fruition in the blink of an eye, it's my superpower. It *will* bring a whole new cross-generational audience to the gallery. It will create media buzz. It will be joyful, and sustainable, and—"

She was losing them. Glazed and fidgety, she could see them pulling back.

The only card she had left to play was the Gilpin card. Something she'd never done before. But she was hoping her parents could bend her way, just a smidge, then surely she could too.

"You know my parents," she said. "They've been on the board here longer than some of you have been alive. They brought me here, knowing my skill set, knowing my abilities, trusting me to do what had to be done to help the gallery survive—"

A loud knock on the glass wall, hard enough the thing shook, took everyone's attention. It was Mimi, frantically pointing at a mobile phone in her hand.

Petra widened her eyes and mouthed, *I'll call them back.*

Mimi, whose eyes looked about to pop, madly shook her head.

Petra dropped her hands to the table and pushed herself to standing. "Excuse me, folks. It seems we've landed in the midst of a pantomime."

The management team laughed politely, or in relief that she'd no longer be badgering them, and Petra excused herself to meet Mimi in the hall.

"Is the building on fire?" Petra asked.

Mimi turned her phone to face Petra, and then began to scroll.

A series of grainy images slid up the page. A bar. A chandelier. Selfies of smiling, happy, drunken people. At the Gilded Cage. Yes, she'd seen all this.

But then the images moved on to what looked like a private room. Studded red velvet walls, gold velvet couches, a mini chandelier, drinks and snacks laid out on a small table. All of this seen through a door left slightly ajar.

And inside Sawyer in his battered leather jacket, his jaw covered in stubble. And she in her pink tulle-skirted dress, her hair a little wild, her shoes tossed onto the couch.

The next shot—she was holding Sawyer's hand. Her other hand touching her chest as she grinned at him. Grinned *down* at him.

Since he was *down on one knee*.

And just like that the floodgates opened, and

image after image from the night at the Gilded Cage came swarming back to her.

Begging the DJ to play Prince and Kylie and the Bee Gees.

Someone suggesting karaoke.

Sawyer saying, "Leave it to us," then holding her hand as he led her through the crowd to a private room he'd nabbed at the flick of a wrist because he owned the place.

Then a beat, a moment, a window in the night where everything went quiet. The air felt cool without the crush of people. And she leant against a couch in a private room, filled with such release and joy at having Sawyer all to herself.

Sawyer. All dusty curls and beautifully smiling eyes.

Sawyer, down on one knee, asking her to—

"There's a video too," said Mimi, snapping Petra back to the present, her voice hushed, reverent.

She clicked on a news article—*a news article!*—*Mystery Mistress Revealed in Exclusive! Heiress to Society Couple Sweeps Billionaire Bachelor Off His Feet! Literally!*

It was so close to the headline Sawyer had joked about, her knees nearly gave out.

And Mimi kept on scrolling. Then, stopping on a video, she clicked.

In the video—taken sneakily, seedily, through the half-open door of the private karaoke room—Sawyer dropped to his knee, held out his hand, while Petra stood barefoot, swaying and smiling so widely she was sure she'd never looked so happy.

"And—?" said Mimi.

"There's an *and*?" Petra asked.

"Your mother keeps calling."

Petra checked her watch, on which she'd set Do Not Disturb during the meeting, to find that, yes, her mother had called. And messaged. As had Deena. A number of media sites had emailed. Even a top wedding dress designer, with the subject line *Symbiotic Opportunity*, which she assumed meant they wanted to offer her a free dress so long as she promoted the heck out of them. Along with a bunch of numbers she didn't recognise.

She stopped only when she found a message from Sawyer. He'd pinned an address. Nothing else. As if he knew that what they had to say to one another had to be said in person.

"Petra?"

She spun to find the gallery manager poking her head around the door.

"Sorry to interrupt, but we do have to get back to the floor before the gallery opens—"

"Right. Of course." Petra gave the tablet to Mimi, who patted her on the arm, her expression saying *You've got this, boss*.

Petra walked back into the conference room to find the others huddled over their phones. As one, they looked up.

The assistant manager, a guy around Petra's age, said, "Is it inappropriate to admit I had such a crush on your fiancé when I was a kid?"

Get in line, Petra thought, laughter gathering at the back of her throat. Then, *My fiancé?*

She opened her mouth to deny all.

Then remembered Sawyer's adage. *"Never deny—no matter how wacky—denial will become the story."*

The last thing the gallery needed was a 'story' taking focus away from the event she was determined to launch.

The term *whiff of scandal* started beating a tattoo inside Petra's head. As if it had been inevitable somehow, from the moment her mother had typed those words. Inevitable that she would disappoint them.

Sawyer warned you this wouldn't magically go away, a voice said, and tut-tutted in the back of her head.

Only she'd been so determined to see him, to do what *she* wanted to do, she might as well have stuck her fingers in her ears and cried, *La-la-la-la-la-la!*

She needed to talk to him. Now.

"I'll let you guys go," Petra said to the room, sounding far calmer than she felt. "Please think over my idea. Any questions, ask. And trust me, I can do this. It will be amazing. And it might just save the gallery."

They all left, smiling and full of beans, where they'd been hesitant and obstructive only minutes earlier.

"I have to go," Petra told Mimi as she hustled to her office.

"No worries. I'll hold the fort." Mimi closed Petra's door and hopped straight on the phone as if nothing had happened.

Petra sent her mother a quick text.

Hey, Mum. Busy now. Talk soon. Don't panic. Everything's fine!

She wondered if she should use all caps to really hit that home.

Then, ignoring all other notifications, she searched her name, and Sawyer's. And there it was—Sawyer dropping to one knee, holding something in his hand. It had been cropped, enhanced like something out of a police procedural TV show.

Petra gasped. Literally. The sound filling her ears. For if nothing else about that shot made any sense to her, one thing sealed it.

She grabbed her handbag, tipped the contents onto her desk and rifled through the detritus till she found what she was looking for.

The small Ziplock bag the dry-cleaner had handed her.

The *pocket stuff.*

And there, inside, the ring pull from the soft drink can.

The one Sawyer was handing her in the pictures. Her engagement ring.

Petra's high heels clacked and wobbled as she strode along the dock looking for the address Sawyer had pinned: the berth number for the Big Think yacht at Melbourne Marina.

A yacht, a nightclub, a graffiti installation/ building, at least a couple of hotels... No wonder the guy didn't need a house, he had a thousand places to stay. And yet he'd stayed with her. Till he hadn't.

Why? That was one of the many burning questions she'd be asking him. *Why did you stay? And why did you leave last night?* And the big one, *Why on earth did you propose to me? Then why not tell me when you had the chance?*

Petra slowed as the berth number neared, then looked up to find herself facing the kind of boat usually only seen in Netflix series about fake heiresses. She'd figured the billionaire thing was some tricksy PR angle, but in that moment realised it must be true.

Discombobulated, overtired and all mixed up inside, she went to yell his name, with gusto, until she saw the name of the yacht. *Candy.* And all the wild thoughts swirling about inside her head quieted.

Candy had been Sawyer's nickname, back in his football days, so good was he at selling fake hand-balls—aka candy to babies—before wrong-footing the opposition and getting clear. The nickname given to him by Finn.

He struggled to talk about her brother, yes, and the way he tried to take Finn's place could be frustrating, but everything pointed to him still feeling the loss in a big way. Which made it hard for her to stay angry at him. People did dumb things when they were hurting.

A flash of something on the top deck caught her eye.

"Sawyer?" she called.

Then there he was, easing around the stern. Decked out in a T-shirt and shorts, his skin tanned and beautiful, his hair ruffled by the sea breeze. If she didn't feel so hamstrung by the whole situation, she might well have swooned.

"What on earth are you wearing?" he asked, as if he was the one who deserved answers!

Petra looked down at her ridiculous get-up, having forgotten she was in disguise. "I borrowed a coat from one of the security guards, and we found a scarf in some leftover merchandise for a Monet exhibition to cover my hair. Then Mimi organised for a car to pick me up from the storage bay so I could get away unseen. By some miracle, it worked."

He gripped the handrail and shielded his eyes from the sun. Was he…? He was laughing!

"None of this is funny!" she cried.

"You're absolutely right."

"We have things to discuss!"

"Then come on up."

She tipped her sunglasses forward, clocked the distance between the bobbing stern and the dock, imagining how her heels might manage it. "Why don't you come down here?"

Sawyer leaned against the railing and squinted her way, as if he was auditioning for an aftershave commercial.

They'd be so lucky, Petra thought, remembering his hand on her cheek, his eyes clouding, all that smoulder focused her way. Before he'd done a runner and ended up on a million-dollar yacht.

Gaze locked onto hers, Sawyer said, "Because out here, on the water, there is a thousand percent higher chance that we can have a conversation without a telephoto lens bearing down on us. And shoes off," he called. "House rules." Before moving to unhitch the boat from its mooring.

Petra, realising she had about half a minute to either join him or be left behind, unzipped her boots, tucked them over her handbag, then hitched her coat and climbed on board.

Sawyer met her up top with a bright yellow safety vest in hand.

"Do I really need that?"

"Humour me," he said. And the heat in his voice, the dark glint in his eye, had her doing as he asked.

Stripping off coat, scarf, sunglasses and dumping her gear in a big pile, she donned the vest over her silk dress, then found herself a seat in the cockpit.

"Can you even drive this thing?" she asked.

"I'm willing to give it a crack," he said, before the rev of engine filled her ears, the deck beneath her swayed as Sawyer nudged them out of the berth, neatly past the line of boats, out of the marina and out to sea, where he really let it rip.

Petra held on tight to the bench beneath her, lifting her hand only to try to get her wildly flapping hair out of her mouth.

While Sawyer looked as if he'd been born on the sea, the creases around his eyes crinkling as he squinted against the light bouncing off the waves, his curls fluttering back off his face. The cotton of his T-shirt pulling tight around his biceps, the edges of one of his many tattoos poking out the bottom, the veins roping down his forearms making her mouth water.

Sawyer looked over his shoulder, as if he'd heard her thoughts.

She waved him to face the front. To watch where they were going.

For, feeling both terrified and strangely ready for it, they were about to have it out. Taking things to a place their friendship had never been before.

But it was time.

* * *

Sawyer pulled back on the rudder, the boat slowing. Then, using lots of fancy radar and autopilot tech, dropped anchor.

After which he leant back against the dash, his feet crossing at the ankles, and looked Petra's way.

The last time she'd been in the same room as him, he'd nearly kissed her. She was *sure* of it. She could still feel the heat of his touch. See the intent in his eyes. Feel the press of her heart against her ribs as it yearned for him.

And now she must look like a crazy person, with clown hair, no shoes and a bright yellow safety vest.

She tugged herself free of the thing, swiped her hair off her face, then said, "I'm assuming, judging by the size of this thing, there's somewhere more civilised we can sit."

Sawyer pointed to a doorway to the right, leading to a set of internal steps.

Petra left her gear upstairs, made her way down. A kitchen took up one end and a large comfortable-looking couch spread bench-style around the outer rim. Smoky blue windows cut out the glare.

"All this," she said, waving an arm around, "is not normal, you do realise that?" Then she plonked onto the couch, the exhaustion of the night before, the importance of the meeting that morning and the shock at finding herself the subject of a viral video finally overwhelming her.

Sawyer leant against the bar, hands gripping the bench. "I'd have come get you—"

"I know," she said, expelling a huff of breath. It must have taken some major self-control for him not to storm the gates and slay the dragon, especially where she was concerned. She appreciated the restraint.

Her gaze swept to his, to find him watching her, his expression wary. Ready for anything. And for the first time since she'd seen the video she wondered how this might all be affecting *him*.

"Are *you* okay?" Petra asked.

He blinked, his lashes bussing his cheeks. "I think you'll find that's my line."

"And yet. Are you?"

"I'll let you know in a minute or two." Because he was waiting on *her*, on her reaction to all that had unfolded that morning. "We know the video came from the puffer jacket guy. We know he contacted a footy journo who declined to pay for the footage. So he found a gossip site that would. We've approached him and found he's all apology and contrition. Sheepish, I believe was the term bandied about. I feel confident we've seen the last of him."

Yes, the video itself was a problem. But she'd put that into a box for later, the implications far too vast for her to imagine. All the space in her head had been taken up with figuring out what the heck had been happening *in* the video in the first place.

She reached into her bag, pulled out the pull tab and flashed it at him as if it were a Watergate tape.

"You kept it," he said, his voice gravelly.

"I didn't *keep* it. The dry-cleaner gave it to me and I forgot to throw it out. For, at the time, I had no idea it had any significance." She curled the strange little artefact back into her hand, as if it was something precious rather than merely evidence. "What were you *thinking*?"

He didn't say.

Which was fine, because Petra wasn't done. "And when I asked you point-blank if anything happened that night, you looked me in the eye and said we just talked."

He shifted a little.

"I know we were in a private room at the time, so there was an expectation of privacy, but you got down on one knee and—" she stopped, swallowed, unable to believe she was about to say the next words "—proposed to me. Using a pull tab. Why? Were you *that* drunk?"

"I was not."

Now he speaks!

Petra raised an eyebrow. "*It's been a long trip. Hard. Tequila, and leave the bottle...*"

"Is that meant to be me?" he asked, his voice low, ominous.

But she was not to be stopped. "Uncanny, right?"

Sawyer's eyes flashed. "I had a couple of shots. Then I stopped. I wasn't about to put myself in a position where I couldn't look out for you."

Petra breathed deeply, and slowly, her voice roiling into a growl, she said, "It's *not* your job to look out for me, Sawyer! What we are to one another, it goes beyond your friendship with Finn, or…or it doesn't work at all."

Otherwise this was all it would ever be: her crushing on him, he protecting her. Now and for ever. And she simply refused to play that game any more.

"Sawyer, I need you to…to respect that I'm fully capable of making my own choices. Making my own mistakes. Dealing with embarrassment. And cleaning up my own messes. All things that I am well-versed in."

Sawyer ran a hand up the back of his neck, looking discomfited. But then he pressed away from the bar, prowled to the couch and sat by her side. Bent over, elbows resting on his knees, he looked to her and said, "You're thirty."

"I'm thirty?" she said. "What has that got to do with…? Do you mean the promise we made at my *eighteenth* birthday party?"

"It came up."

"You mean *I* brought it up?"

A single nod.

Her eighteenth birthday party had been a formal affair, populated by her parents' friends and their kids. The only highlight? Sawyer. Showing up unexpectedly, for the first time in several months, having disentangled himself from her grieving family not long after Finn had died.

High from seeing him, she'd jokingly—or not so jokingly—convinced him to make a 'let's get married if neither of us are by the time I'm thirty' pact. Which neither had brought up again in all the years since. Except she had. At the Gilded Cage. Leading to him getting down on one knee.

Sawyer hadn't told her, because to him it didn't register as important.

Because it wasn't real.

Done, cooked, over and out, Petra sank low in the chair, her legs poking out in front of her, her eyes squeezed shut. Only for the taste of lemon, salt and tequila to suddenly hit the back of her tongue.

"Petra," Sawyer said, his voice deep with anguish. And apology. But she was not having it.

"Shh!" she insisted, holding up a finger as she felt a swell of memories break the surface...

"Do you remember my eighteenth birthday party?" she asked as she leaned against the velvet couch in the private karaoke room.

She was waiting for the hen night girls to join them. Till then, the relative quiet was a relief.

Sawyer stood by the door. "I do."

"Do you remember your gift to me?" said Petra, holding eye contact for all she was worth.

Sawyer's nostrils flared.

In case that was a no, she said, *"If neither of us was married by the time I turned thirty, you'd... do the deed."*

Sawyer coughed out a laugh, but there was no humour in it. In fact, it appeared as if he was masking a measure of pain. *"Were you drinking tequila that night too?"*

"Grapefruit Vodka Cruisers. I thought they were the height of sophistication."

"And now?" he asked.

"Haven't touched one since that night." A pause. *"And I turned thirty last summer."*

She tipped forward, flashing her left hand at him, to prove it was devoid of rings. *"I know,"* she said, *"big shock, right? I mean I have a crazy cool career. I'm well-travelled, I have great taste in movies, I'm cute."*

She awaited confirmation.

"Am I not cute?"

"As a button," he said, a muscle twinging in his cheek. *"Instead of karaoke, how about I see you home?"*

No way was she going home when Sawyer Mahoney had just admitted he thought she was cute. Yes, she'd forced it out of him, the same way she'd forced him to promise to marry her. But still.

"I'm flexible," she said, pressing away from

the couch to tiptoe around the small room, as if she might do a split leap at any moment, only to forget what she was saying when she noticed the fabulous wallpaper and the cool vintage op shop art. "I can't cook, but I'm a champion at take-out. And I have stamina. Like super-human stamina. Just ask Russell."

At that Sawyer looked to the ceiling and seemed to whisper some kind of prayer under his breath.

"You know what?" said Petra, spinning to point a finger Sawyer's way. His face wavered at the end. Or maybe that was her. "I'm a freaking catch!"

Sawyer, who'd been glancing between the exit and Petra, as if readying to step in and rescue her if required, shot his gaze to hers, his eyes dark, strained and...hot. As if he was using copious amounts of energy to fend off her attributes. In case they hit their target. Which was, of course, him.

Sawyer, who smelled like a summer storm. And apples. And leather. And kindness. Did kindness have a smell? Sawyer, who made her feel all the feely feelings.

No other man had made her feel that way. Not the shy taxidermist. Not the drummer who was obsessed with the pre-Raphaelites. The good men, the loud men, the arty men. She'd tried them all on for size, hoping one might stand out, might see some stray pink found thing and think of her.

"I'm never going to find someone," she said, "and it's all your fault."

"Petra..." he said, his voice wary.

And through her fuzzy gaze she saw him start to think, to put two and two together. Meaning soon he'd figure out that she'd been in love with him for sixteen-odd years.

Her chest tightened. She started to panic.

She blurted, "The promise! What if it's the promise holding me back? Like it's a curse. Or there's some psychological block stopping me from finding my person."

Outside the small room Kylie sang about spinning around. While inside the room Sawyer looked at her as if he believed her. And she found herself counting down to the moment he bolted for the door.

Instead, he dropped to one knee.

Petra's hands flew up in the air. "What are you doing?"

"Breaking the curse," he said.

Then he leapt back up again. Or stood with a wince, considering his old injury. Found a can on the coffee table and twisted off the pull tab. Sank slowly back to one knee and held the "ring" on the palm of his hand.

Petra's senses sharpened, as if she'd sobered up quite a bit.

Then everything seemed to slow, to unfurl, as Sawyer's deep, husky voice said, "Petra Gilpin, will you do me the honour of fulfilling the promise we made all those years ago, when you were young and knew no better, and tipsy on Vodka Cruisers, and say that you will marry me?"

Petra opened her mouth to answer, only to find her mouth was already open and no sound was coming out.

Sawyer went on, "After which you will rightly change your mind, so that the curse of the promise is broken and you can get on with your life. Unhindered. Open to find your person." A quick smile. A heartbreaking smile. Then, "What say you?"

Feeling silly, and more than a little hurt—mostly by herself for letting it get that far, Petra grabbed Sawyer by the hand and hauled him back to stand.

Just as Deena and the hen night girls piled into the room.

Petra fluttered her eyes open to find she was still on the yacht, muted sunlight slanting through the tinted windows.

Sawyer had gone down on one knee to break the curse of a promise he'd made all those years before, so that she could feel free to love someone else.

If she hadn't known what heartbreak felt like before that moment, she knew now.

CHAPTER SEVEN

IN THAT MOMENT Petra felt a clarity she'd not felt since she'd arrived back home, as the entirety of her situation unspooled before her.

Taking on a job she was not fit to do, in the hope of finding some connection with her parents. And throwing herself in Sawyer's path, in the hopes he'd see how important he was to her.

All of which was now out there, in the public domain, for anyone and everyone to pick apart at their leisure.

It was all such a mess that she began to laugh. Till her eyes streamed and her stomach hurt. Till she wondered if she might, in fact, be falling apart.

Sawyer slid along the couch till his thigh bumped hers, his hand landing on the back of her neck gently, warmly, sending goosebumps skittering all over her already fraught body.

No, he didn't get to do that to her unless he meant it. She sat up and shook him off, turning to face him with an accusing finger keeping him at bay.

"You pretend proposed to me because of some silly joke made years ago."

Not a joke.

"In order to break my bad dating curse."

Not a curse.

"But I never actually said yes."

Why hadn't she said yes? Some latent self-protective instinct that had beaten the tequila?

For a second she felt fiercely proud, while also terribly bereft.

"Which matters not a jot, for the whole world *thinks* we're engaged. Which we can't deny, because that will somehow only make it more true."

Sawyer held up a hand and said, "May I speak?"

Petra's glare could have burned holes in his clothes. But then she'd be dealing with glimpses of Sawyer's bare chest, and the last thing she needed to add to the mix was Sawyer-lust. Which, despite being upset with him right now, never seemed to go away.

"Forget about the video," he said. "Forget about that whole night. We were, neither of us, at our most lucid. So I suggest we give ourselves a break, let that go down in flaming history, and figure out what to do from here." A beat then, "How does that sound to you?"

It sounded…like a good place to start. She nodded and said, "Fine. So what's the plan?"

"You tell me."

Right. So this was where her *I'm fully capable of making my own mistakes* speech came back to bite her. That was quick. But at least he was lis-

tening. Trusting her to take the lead. Reminding
her that he *was* on her side.

"Where do I even start?" she relented.

"What do you want, Petra? What do you want
to get out of this? What do you want to happen?"

"I want," she said, "to be able to do what I'm
really damn good at, without anyone looking over
my shoulder and judging how I go about it."

He nodded. "So, what can we do to facilitate
that?"

"We control the narrative."

A smile shot across his face, and she softened
towards him a little more. Despite how much easier it made things to think that way, Sawyer was
not the bad guy here. They were truly mixed up
in this thing together.

He sat back, his knee shifting to point her way,
his meaty arm resting along the back of the couch.
"So, what's our story?"

"It's not what it looks like? Just a drunken mis-
understanding?"

"We can go that way. Sure. If you think you can
smooth things over with the gallery, I can deal
with Hadley. Or?"

"Or," she said, warming to this now, "I could
push you overboard. Or smother you with one of
these cushions. Then everyone will feel sorry for
me and give me everything I want."

A grin. The kind that shot straight to her middle and lit a fire deep down inside. "That's a story

all right. Unfortunately for you, my survival instincts are pretty good. I'd fight back. Any other ideas?"

Just one. The most dicey one. The one she was sure—considering past actions—would send him jumping overboard without need of a push.

"We honour the original promise."

Something flickered behind his gaze, as if he'd been expecting it. All of it. All along. And he'd been patiently waiting for her to come to the same conclusion.

"We remain," she set out, just in case he wasn't following along, "for all intents and purposes engaged. Until some cat is born that barks like a dog and we become old news. Then we gently go back to the way things were before."

"Right," he said, with a finality that she felt scoot down her spine.

"*Right* as in you would buy a poster starring the Barking Cat, considering your affinity for such things, or *right* as in...the rest."

His smile was smoother that time. More focused. "All of the above."

"Really?" she asked, her voice kicking high. "You'd do that? For me?"

He cocked his head, as if to say, *Petra, I'd do anything for you. And if you don't know that by now, then you've not been paying attention.*

Feeling it now, how it might work, how it could make all the *whiff of scandal* stuff go away, she turned to face him, her knee bumping his as it swept up onto the couch. "There is a lot *not* to like about the idea. We'd be lying, for one thing. To our families, our friends, our workplaces. I just… I don't think I can do that."

"It doesn't have to be a lie."

Petra's heart forgot itself for a beat, seizing up, before slamming against her ribs. "Meaning… what, exactly?"

He held out his hand. When she stared at it, he wriggled his fingers and said, "Gimme the ring."

She opened her hand to find the pull tab still tucked up safely inside.

Sawyer plucked it from her palm. Then eased himself off the couch and onto the floor, where he landed. On one knee.

"Oh, get up!" Petra said, rearing back, her voice echoing around the small space. "Seriously. It was ill-thought-out the first time and now you're just being ridiculous."

But he remained there, kneeling before her, looking strangely at ease. Sawyer the knight in shining armour, in his element. Then he held up the pull tab, twisting it back and forth so that it caught the light.

And despite the fact that it had been yanked from a random can at a bar, she found herself captured. By the enormity of his offer, the deference with which he'd gone about it, and the talisman itself. This strange, sharp-edged thingamajig that had no meaning to anyone but them. Which made it a thing of beauty in itself.

"Petra Gilpin," he said, his voice sombre, his expression fierce, "will you do me the honour of agreeing to be my fiancée?" Then, "Till the time comes when it's no longer necessary to pretend."

She knew what he meant, but for a blissful few moments her brain took his words a very different way.

Drunk, bolshie and high on lemon pulp, she'd managed to protect herself from a moment such as this. Now, in the cold light of day, she found the wherewithal to say, "I have one provision. You can't do what you did last night."

His gaze flared. And for a moment she wondered if he thought she was referring to the near kiss.

"By that," she explained, "I mean you can't just leave, not without warning. Not without reason. I mean, you can do as you please, because you are your own person, and this will all be pretend. Just... I'd appreciate it if you could give me a heads-up, and some context, so that I don't worry."

And don't consistently feel like it's my fault that you go.

Sawyer breathed out hard through his nose. "Were you truly worried last night?"

"I wasn't, because I'm aware that you can handle yourself. And yet I was."

Because I wasn't entirely sure if you'd come back.

"So long as we're in this I won't go far, not without notice. Fair?"

"Fair."

"So, what'll it be?"

Which was how, the second time Sawyer Mahoney got down on one knee to ask Petra Gilpin to marry him, she let him slide the pull tab onto the tip of her finger, for the thing was not built to go past a knuckle, and she said, "Fine. What the heck."

"What the heck?" Sawyer repeated, clearly bemused.

Petra coughed out a laugh, feeling as if all the tension inside her had been replaced by helium. "Well, what did you expect me to say? *Yes! A thousand times, yes*?"

"That level of enthusiasm wouldn't go amiss." Wincing, Sawyer pressed his hand onto his thigh to find leverage to get himself back up.

"Your leg!" said Petra, reaching to help him up onto the couch, dragging him so that he sat right by her. Her skirt caught under his thigh, her hand hooked around his arm. Their faces danger close.

"Seriously," she said on an exhalation of breath that shifted the hair by his ear. "The one knee thing was not necessary."

"Except now, when anyone asks, we can tell the truth—I fell to one knee and begged you to be mine."

"You didn't have to beg all that hard."

His eyes swept over hers, and she wondered if he saw the truth behind the joke. Saw how being this close to him messed with her completely.

"I mean, come on," she said, doing her best to keep things light. "I'm now officially fake-engaged to one of the *Top Ten Sexiest Single Billionaire Bachelors Under Forty Alive!* Or maybe they didn't have to be alive… I can't remember."

Sawyer laughed, though it sounded far more as if he was in pain.

"Truly, though," she said, using her hand at his elbow to yank him a little closer, the feel of him all up in her space making everything else feel secondary, "I am so grateful to you, Sawyer Mahoney. Grateful that you are good-looking enough that people might *actually* believe I'd want to marry you."

"Is that right?" he said, and something changed in his gaze. As if one second he was Sawyer Mahoney, the next he was *Sawyer Mahoney.* Bringing her right back to the night before, his hand on her face, the *certainty* that he'd wanted to kiss her.

And she wondered—just how far *would* he go for her?

If she wanted to touch him, would he let her? If she moved to kiss him, would he lean in? He shifted on the seat, adjusting himself, and she knew. Knew in that deep, most feminine place that all she had to do was ask.

"What is going on in that head of yours?" he asked, his voice deep.

Petra felt completely hollow now. As if she was made of the most delicate shell. But she managed to say, "Watch many Netflix romances, do you?"

His surprise at the change of subject was clear. "Not a lot of time for Netflix on the road."

"Imagine a princess who's not really a princess, who becomes fake engaged to a carpenter who's actually a prince. For terribly good reasons. Only now they have to decide how far they'll go, in public, to sell the story."

She licked her bottom lip and Sawyer's gaze moved to her mouth. Where it stayed.

His voice was rough as he said, "Still no idea what you're talking about."

"They must agree, the non-princess and the carpenter prince, the boundaries of their fake relationship. Enough to convince the world that the relationship is true, not so much either party feels uncomfortable."

"Define 'so much'," Sawyer said. Then he shifted again, dragging the edge of her swishy silk skirt underneath him more, so that her legs were bare from her chipped pink toenails to halfway up her thigh.

Which he noticed, she noticed, the whites of his eyes turning to smoke.

"Okay," she managed, even as her skin began to flame, her breath now hard to come by. "Do they make goo-goo eyes at one another? Do they hold hands? Do they…?" She took a quick breath.

"Do they kiss? If so, is there a time-limit on the kiss? Do they—?"

"Who are we talking about again?" Sawyer asked, his eyes so dark she could barely make out the colour.

"The non-princess," said Petra, her voice cracking. "And the carpenter prince. They have to prove they don't hate one another, remember?"

"Right. But I don't think anyone would ever accuse the two of us of *hating* one another."

An innocuous claim, only the way he said it made it feel as if it was crystal-clear to the whole wide world that they felt something very different from hate.

"So this is about *us* now?" she asked.

His gaze returned to hers, and the little finger of the hand at the end of the arm she still held began to trace circles on her bare thigh. "Petra, it's always been about us."

And Petra nearly expired on the spot.

"So," she said, "what do we do? To convince everyone we're—" She paused when she felt the lift of his chest, so close to hers now they nearly touched.

"Madly in love?" Sawyer finished.

"Well," she said, "I was going to say convince everyone we're hot and heavy behind closed doors, but sure. Let's go with madly in love."

He laughed, the rough sound vibrating through her, his breath rushing over her hair. He was so close now, every time she breathed she caught the scent of him. She wished she could run her fingers over his cheek, his jaw, his lips. Or her lips. Tasting him. As if simply finding out if he was as warm and tough as he looked would fulfil her for the rest of time.

"Do you think," she said, "that we can pull it off?"

The moment felt like a soap bubble—precious and precarious—and she wanted it to go on for ever.

"Yeah," he said, brushing the back of his hand against the edge of her skirt, before his hand landed on her knee. "I reckon we can."

Petra had never let herself believe there was the remotest chance that he felt for her the way she felt for him. If she had, she'd never have dated, much less tried to muddle her way through a relationship. She'd have been doomed to a life lived alone, without even the chance of reprieve.

But what if he *did* feel the same way she did? All this—the sleepovers, the massages, the hair play, the hot glances, the touching, the near kiss, the proposal, the second proposal... Surely that added up to something? Something bigger than she'd allowed herself to believe?

"On that note," she said, before she lost her nerve, her voice barely above a whisper, "last night, before you felt a sudden need to go water a horse, I got the feeling that… That you wanted to kiss me."

There, bomb dropped. Whatever happened from here, that could not be unsaid. Good. Great! It was about time!

Except Sawyer said nothing.

Petra, already rolling downhill, added, "I want you to know, for the sake of the current conversation, that I'd have been amenable to that. If that were, in fact, the case."

Nothing. Only the dark clouds in his eyes, the stroke of his thumb over her thigh.

"Now's really not the moment to go all stoic on me, Sawyer," she said, her voice croaky. Her need for him to meet her halfway verging on panic. "Tell me I was wrong. Or tell me I was right."

She could see the argument going on behind his eyes. *Years'* worth of convincing himself that she was Finn's little sister warring against the attraction that had pulled them together, till she was a heartbeat away from curling up on his lap.

Then he shook his head slowly back and forth. Only she knew it wasn't a *No, I feel nothing for you* shake but a *Petra, do you know what you're asking?* shake.

The slow build, the fast burn, the years of yearning. It all pulsed within her. And she knew that if this wasn't going to happen when she was engaged to the guy, then it was never going to happen at all.

"Screw it," Petra said and, grabbing Sawyer by the shirt front with both hands, she dragged him to her and planted a kiss on his mouth.

Direct hit. So unexpected to the both of them, their teeth clashed, just a little.

While Petra winced, Sawyer did not react, not in the optimal way a man might act after finding himself kissed.

He. Did. Not. Kiss. Her. Back.

Seconds slunk by. Two, maybe three. Or maybe a hundred. An interminable amount of time in which Petra regretted every decision that had led her to this moment. A feeling that worsened when her eyes sprang open to find his staring into hers.

Oh, God...oh, God...oh, God.

What had she done?

There was no taking this back! No jetlag or tequila to blame. No amount of pretending in the world that could make this go away. Mortified, devastated, she made to pull back, her breath rushing past her lips and over his on a ragged, aching sigh—

Then Sawyer's eyes slammed closed, his hand dived into the back of her hair and he angled the kiss, slanting his mouth over hers with the most perfect, soft, warm seal that had ever existed on planet Earth.

He wanted this! He wanted her!

Telling herself to stop thinking and just *be*, for this might *never* happen again, Petra let herself let go. Let every feeling she'd ever felt for him rush to the surface, filling her with sweetness, and magic, and joy.

Sawyer's arms slid around her waist, pulling her close, spinning her up and onto his lap. Till they were entwined round one another, clothes twisted, hands lost in touching one another.

And his kisses, those drugging kisses, took her down, down, down—till she could barely see for the fog.

Needing more, needing all of him, she shifted, turned, tucked her knees either side of his hips. Her hands reached for the hem of his shirt, lifting, yanking, till she found skin.

All that hot, hard, smooth, glorious skin. She traced his ribs, his sides, the rough of his tattoos, the whorls of hair on his chest.

And when her hand dived to the waistband of his shorts he rasped, "Hold on," against her hot mouth.

But she didn't want to hold on. She wanted to keep going. Forward. No looking back. Sinking down into his lap, her centre notched to his. His… hard, hot, ready centre, pressing against the seam of his shorts. Pressing against her.

And they pulled apart as one. Their eyes met. Wild and reckless.

His were asking, *Are we really doing this?*

She answered with a roll of her hips, her teeth biting down on her bottom lip to hold in the moan.

Breathing out hard, Sawyer used both hands to press back her hair. Then, holding her face, he pressed a soft kiss to her mouth. To each cheek. To each eyelid.

Then, with her eyes still closed, he kissed his way down her neck, easing the loose neck of her soft dress aside as he grazed his teeth over her collarbone.

Then, with the utmost care, he dragged one shoulder free as he nuzzled his nose over the edge of her lace bra, his teeth grabbing the edge and pulling it down, down. Till she felt the waft of his warm breath over her exposed breast, a moment before his mouth closed over her nipple.

And there he remained for the longest time, tasting, licking, biting, sucking. Learning her breaths, her gasps, what made her roll against him as she chased the pleasure he gave.

He licked his way across to the other side, tugging her shirt so that her arms were now pinned to her sides, before yanking the bra cup aside and sucking her breast into his mouth.

She cried out, no amount of lip-biting could hold her back.

When the pleasure built inside her so thick, so rushed, so wild that she thought she might finish from his kisses alone, she managed to lift her arms enough to cradle his head and drag his mouth back to hers.

Sawyer lifted her from the couch in one easy

move, as if she weighed nothing, as if she gave him superhuman strength. Then they were moving through the lounge.

She could sense the boat around them—the tight furniture, the lull of the water, the angled walls. But she trusted Sawyer to navigate it. To protect her.

She hitched herself higher, wrapped her legs around his waist. One hand thrust into her hair as he kissed her as if she was the very air he needed, his other hand held her backside, her skirt and the flimsiest of underwear all that kept him from touching her where she wanted him to touch her most.

Inside a double bedroom, he tossed her to the bed. She landed, she bounced and she laughed, the sound echoing off tinted windows with a view of sky and ocean and nothing else.

Then she realised that she was alone on the bed.

Sawyer was standing at the end, his hair a mess, his T-shirt skew-whiff, the evidence of his desire tenting his shorts in such a way her mouth went dry.

She could see him overthinking, see him second-guessing. Was he really about to pull a Sawyer and do the right thing, putting an end to it all?

"Stay with me," she said, lifting up onto her elbows. Not a request, a demand. "I *want* this." Then, in case he needed it to be as clear as it was possible for it to be, she braved up and added, "I've always wanted this."

She let her knee fall to one side, her dress sliding down her thigh. His gaze dropped, the heat therein enough to scorch her from head to toe.

Then he tugged off his shirt, in that seriously sexy back to front way men used, and she felt so happy, so overjoyed, she lay back on the bed and laughed.

The bed moved as Sawyer climbed into the end, crawling up her body till he rested on his hands over the top of her. His face was so close she could count the three perfect freckles beneath his left eye, the tangle of lashes, the rough scrape of stubble on his beautiful jaw.

And that bare chest, with the wings of the phoenix tattoo that covered his upper back curling over both shoulders. Myriad tattoos, curling and merging over that warm brown skin, some hidden beneath swirls of coarse dark hair. It was all she could do not to growl.

Hooking her foot around his backside, she pulled him to her, eyes fluttering as his centre met hers. Then he moved, so that they could fit together more fully, and so that he didn't crush her with his bulk.

Then he leaned in and brushed his lips over hers. Gently. Sweetly. Tasting her. Taking her lower lip between his and tugging.

She felt drugged. Loose. Limp. Her skin on fire. When her mouth popped open on a sigh he took advantage, covering her mouth with his, his tongue sweeping inside.

She used her leg around his backside to press herself closer, to rub against him, to give herself some relief. Before his kisses sent her swirling into madness.

Then he moved away, enough that she grabbed for him.

"It's okay," he promised, a smile in his voice, and wonder and heat. "Just evening the score."

With that he peeled her dress down her arms and over her hips, his skin rough, his hands gentle. His gaze fierce as he drank her in.

Then it was hot damp skin on hot damp skin. Hands everywhere. The taste of his skin in her mouth as she dragged her teeth over his shoulder in a way that had him crying out. And pressing himself against her in a way that sent her mind blank with pleasure.

Somehow they were both naked, protected, and when he kissed her then there was no holding back. No thought, just feeling. Touch. Worship. Chasing one another's sighs and gasps.

No boundaries, no questions, just raw feeling and relief.

Till Petra was gone. Lost to sensation. All the feelings she'd ever felt for this man rolling through her like a summer storm.

And when it broke, when *she* broke, it was wild, and vast, and inevitable.

CHAPTER EIGHT

Sheet half falling off the too-small bed, one arm crooked behind his head, the other hand unconsciously tracing the tattoos covering his left pec, Sawyer lay back and stared at the panelled ceiling of the cabin.

He could almost feel the rocking of the waves if he concentrated hard enough. Though concentration was nearly impossible with the sound of the shower just behind the bathroom door. His mind playing out every move he imagined Petra making as she took that shower.

He pulled himself to sitting and ran both hands over his face. Hard. Trying to pin down some crummy feeling that he could grip onto. Shame? Disappointment? Only he felt none of them. Not a lick.

From the moment he'd seen Petra standing on the jetty looking so damned adorable in that oversized coat, dark sunglasses, scarf around her head, he'd felt as if some inevitable force had finally caught up with him.

The fake engagement, play-acting how that might look and finally, *finally*, kissing her, holding her, tasting her, taking her to his bed, he'd almost seen it unfold before it even happened. As if it had been written in the stars.

But, for all that, he *had* crossed a line. A line he'd been nudging for years.

Every time he'd waved to her in the stands of a youth football game. Or sought her out in the gardens of her family home, offering to carry her collections, when he was meant to be hanging with Finn.

At her eighteenth birthday party, having gone specifically to apologise for not being around after Finn died. Only to see her and feel as if his twenty-year-old heart had been blown wide open.

Then that crazy night at the Gilded Cage.

After years spent keeping himself in check, it had taken one night to screw it all up. As if everything he knew about responsibility and duty had fled his head as soon as she'd hit him with that smile.

He'd been treading water ever since. Not sure if he was coming or going. There was a limit to how long a man could hold out under that pressure. And he'd finally reached his.

It was the only way he could make sense of their conversation the night before. When she'd asked about his dreams. His passions. What one thing he'd do with his life if he was given the chance.

And he'd told her the truth. That he had no

dream of his own. Something he'd never really admitted to himself, much less out loud.

But rather than feeling as if his foundation had been pulled out from under him, it had been a relief to say so. A relief to tell her. The truth had set him free.

Leaving room for more truths to rise to the surface. Specifically how lovely she'd looked, sitting on the lounge room floor, her shirt half falling off one shoulder, her dark auburn hair pulled back off her face, leaving her with nowhere to hide. The attraction she felt written in every swallow, every flicker in those big hazel eyes.

He felt punch-drunk simply being with her. And now he'd not only walked over the line, he'd demolished it completely.

A bump came from the bathroom. Followed by an oath. The shower wasn't big, as he'd discovered when he'd fled there the night before, as his last thread of self-control had begun to fray.

And, crossed line or not, he wanted to join her there. So badly he ached. He rearranged himself over the sheet, his hand staying where it was. Cupping himself. As if he might be able to hypnotise the thing into submission.

His brain wasn't helping, flashing up memories of her pink cheeks, her mouth open, her eyes hooded, back arched, her hair trailing over her bare breasts as she straddled him.

Gritting his teeth, he left *himself* alone, hauled himself to standing and paced.

He'd not join her in the shower. She needed space. Time. To think. To decide how she felt about all that had happened.

She already knew how *he* felt about it. Screwed. In every way imaginable.

Engaged—to Petra. Sleeping with Petra. Imagining ways he could actually make this work, with Petra. After spending a lifetime determined to keep her from harm, the only reason she was in this mess in the first place was because of him.

And all because of an ancient birthday promise...

It was a year or so since Finn's death when Sawyer opened the invitation, splayed out on the busted mattress in his university dorm room, paid for by a football scholarship that was looking precarious after his having asked the Dean for yet another shift in major.

The snick of the envelope, the feel of the card— a soft, buttery pink, the paper like linen over silk—was like something out of another life.

So, having not seen the Gilpins for some months, after having slowly, regretfully, necessarily disentangled himself from their all-consuming grief, he walked up the front steps of their stately Brighton house to the sound of a jazz quartet spilling across the manicured front lawn, the sight of golden lanterns lighting the way to the huge back yard. Neither of which seemed at all like choices the messy-haired, slow-blinking, sweet-smiling Petra he knew would have made.

So he wasn't surprised to see dozens of people in their fifties and sixties—no doubt business associates of the elder Gilpins—as well as a hundred-odd rowdy teens, dancing beneath a marquee, leaping into the pool, taking advantage of an impressive champagne fountain.

Then a shaft of moonlight fell on a willowy young woman talking to a group of suits. She wore a pale peach dress that began with a big bow gathered behind her neck and then floated around her to her ankles. Her long, smooth auburn hair was gathered in a braid over one shoulder.

It took him more than a second to realise it was the birthday girl. But his reaction to seeing her again was visceral. He felt it in his gut, behind his ribs, in the sweat of his palms, and deeper.

She took a sip of her drink and looked around. As if searching for something. Or someone.

Till her eyes found him.

Pale hazel eyes made vibrant by the moonlight and clever make-up widened. Her wide mouth fell open. Then, with a squeal, she hitched up her dress and ran across the yard.

"Sawyer! Oh, my God!"

Then she was in his arms, having thrown herself there and holding on tight.

"Thank heavens you're here. I wasn't certain you'd come."

His arms wrapped about her, holding her tight lest her momentum take them both down. "Of course I came."

She nodded into his neck. Her hair tickled his nose. Her skin felt like velvet against the roughness of his cheek. His hands dipped into the very real curves at her waist and her breasts pressed into his chest.

She smelled drinkable. There was no other word for it.

His heart beat a hard, fast, telling tattoo behind his ribs as he slowly led her to the grass, uncurled his arms from around her and shoved his hands in his pockets.

"Nice party," he said.

She pulled a face. "This has nothing to do with me," she said. "Clearly. But when they offered... after the past year, how could I say no?"

Sawyer nodded, the lump in his throat stopping any actual words from coming forth. For the loss of Finn still raged inside him. The unfairness of it all.

"I'll be at the same uni as you soon," she said. "You're looking at a Fine Arts major."

"Good for you," he said, his mind spinning to what it would be like, seeing her around campus.

He imagined her knocking on his dorm room

door. Barefoot, hair loose, an eighteen-year-old's smile on her face.

"Ah!" he said. "But we might just be ships passing in the night."

"You're leaving uni?"

He'd not considered it seriously till that moment. "I'm thinking of entering the rookie draft."

His coaches were pushing him. And his teammates. And the state league organisers who couldn't understand why the consistent Best and Fairest wasn't out there. But it felt wrong, because Finn would never get the chance.

Would Petra think so too?

Her mouth popped open, her big eyes grew wide. Then she smacked him on the arm. "Sawyer, that's brilliant!"

"Yeah..." he said, and the idea now hooked in his gut.

His sisters were all doing okay. His mother loved having her first grandchild to help look after. Maybe this was the right time to do something for himself.

"It's been your dream for as long as I've known you," said Petra. "Yours and Finn's. You have to do it. Do it for him."

Her words rocketed around his chest like an out-of-control firework. The weight of responsibility settled back over him like an oft-worn cloak.

She lifted her bottle—some kind of vodka

mixer—to her mouth as she looked about at the party, her glossy lips leaving a soft pink smudge on the rim.

"So, which one of those meatheads is your boy-friend?" Sawyer asked, needing to say something. "I'll need to give him a good talking-to."

Her left eyebrow kicked into a point. "I think you're mistaking me for someone else."

So, no boyfriend... Good. "Girlfriend, then?"

She grinned and shook her head. "I'm not their type. Any of them. Not cool enough. Or stylish enough. Nor do I know enough about stocks or stats and markets to keep up with them. But that's just fine, as none of them are my type either."

And something in her gaze, a level of adult knowledge, had him looking away.

Gutless, the voice inside his head spoke up.

He squished it before it could draw another breath. This had nothing to do with a game. Or intent. She and her parents were only just emerging from the worst of their grief. It was impor-tant he keep himself removed from that. For his sake, and for hers.

Then there was the fact he'd never let on to Finn about the feelings he had for his little sister. Never gauged whether they'd have his friend's blessing, figuring they had time. For her to grow up and for him to make sure he was worthy of her.

Sawyer reached out as a waiter passed, grab-bing another pink bottle for Petra.

Petra deftly popped her empty bottle on the tray of the next waiter and grabbed him a can of beer. His favourite. And he wondered if that was why it was on offer.

Lifting the pull tab with a click and a swish, Petra took a sip from the can, then handed him the rest, her kiss mark right there, where his mouth would go.

He took a quick sip to get it over with. Then, with nervous tension riding high, he bounced the pull tab on his hand—palm, back of hand, palm, back of hand. A habit from his footy days, staying dexterous.

Watching his hand, Petra said, "I do wonder, though. What if I die, never having had a boyfriend?"

"Petra..." he said, unable to tell if it was warning or want grazing the edge of his tone.

"No, truly—what if I don't? It could happen. What if some disease takes out half the men on the planet? Or climate change means we all live in caves and I never get to meet anyone—?"

"If all of that actually happens then I'll help you. Somehow. Okay?"

She nodded, as if that was what she'd been asking of him all along. Then she said, "Now, where's my present?"

"Ah... My presence is the best gift of all."

"Hmm..." she said, eyes narrowed. Then she laughed, as if she'd known it somehow. Known

him. That he was a show-up kind of guy rather than a pepper-with-trinkets kind of guy.

Only now he had the feeling that she'd been leading him to this point the whole time.

"How about we come up with something I want that only you can provide?" She tapped a finger to her lips.

And for a second Sawyer thought she was asking him to kiss her. For another second he wondered if he had it in him to refuse.

"I know!" she said. "How about if neither of us are married by the time I turn thirty you marry me?"

It took him a moment to pivot, before he burst out laughing.

Petra did not join him. In fact she reared back as if...as if he'd slapped her.

"Whoa! Wait... You don't mean that."

Realising his reaction had not been what she'd hoped for, he shot out his spare hand, touching her waist, his fingers dipping into the fabric till her warmth seeped through. He moved his hand to her elbow instead.

She glared at him. Said, "I mean it with every fibre of my being."

Then she hiccupped. And his panic eased. A little.

"Why?" he asked.

When what he meant was, Why me?

For he was a mess. He'd missed the draft the

year he'd been meant to enter, pulling out after Finn's death. Since then he'd struggled to find any real purpose at uni. And he was still looking after his mum and sisters, who were becoming more work as they grew up rather than less.

"Why not?" she said, reaching out to touch his arm.

"I think it's the pink fizzy drink talking."

"It's not," she said, her voice now a little hoarse. "It's something I think about. A lot."

At that she lifted her chin, as if daring him to make fun. Then she shivered, goosebumps springing up all over her arms. And he realised that he still had his hand on her elbow, while hers was on his arm.

He slid his hand away. Only he took the long way round, his fingers tracing her bare arm, finding her skin so smooth and warm beneath his football-roughened palm. When his hand reached hers it was facing upward, her impossibly pale skin catching the moonlight, showing the vulnerable trace of veins beneath the surface of her wrist.

Then her hand was in his.

His, a voice reiterated inside his head.

He let her go and said, "Sure. If that's what you want for your birthday. If you and I are both single, free and clear, without even a hope of a relationship on the horizon by the time you turn thirty, let's get hitched."

"Yes!" she said, grabbing his hand and yanking him close.

So close he could see the swirl of greens and greys dancing in her eyes. So close he could almost taste her scent on the back of his tongue. That heady, wild, warm, drinkable scent.

"We can travel," she said, "and go on adventures, and eat too much, and seek out amazing little galleries in remote places. Or find some fabulous little place with a view and stay in bed all day long. And it'll be fabulous."

He started bouncing the can's pull tab on his hand again, trying to keep the image of staying in a bed with her all day long from embedding itself in his brain.

Petra caught the silver ring in mid-air and shot him a grin. Then she bounced it on her own palm, saying the letters of the alphabet along with each bounce.

"What are you doing?" he asked.

"Shh..." she said, frowning as the thing missed her hand and fell to the grass.

She picked it up and did the same on the back of her hand. Starting the alphabet under her breath again.

"I'm figuring out the initials of my future husband. Did you never play that game as a kid?"

The pull tab fell. She picked it up and tucked it into her palm.

"And?" he asked.

"Turns out you're off the hook," she said, handing the pull tab back to him. "I'll be marrying some lucky guy with the initials XO. Still, just in case, you're my backup."

He lifted his can, and she clinked it with her bottle. And they smiled at one another over their drinks. As if they both knew, somehow, that if this XO guy came along Sawyer would send him packing.

And in that perfect moment, with zing and spark swirling around them, it felt like a dance. Like no one else needed him.

Not his sisters. Not his teammates. Not even Finn.

Only her.

Sawyer pocketed the pull tab and listened as she told him about her degree, and her plan to eventually move to Paris and steep herself in coffee and paint dust and become a world-famous artist. Or a curator if it turned out she had zero talent.

She rocked from side to side as she spoke, so that her dress swished about her legs, hugging her lithe curves before floating out again.

It brought back another memory. Another time. Of her standing in the doorway of Finn's bedroom, with the boys on the floor doing homework—aka predicting the end-of-year AFL ladder to see if their favourite team, the Collin-

gwood Magpies, might make it—asking if they'd like some snacks.

It was as if someone had shot a hose filled with cold water at the back of Sawyer's neck.

This was Petra. Finn's. Little. Sister. He'd been promising to marry her in some distant dystopian future when what he should have been promising was to fill the hole in her life Finn had left behind.

He decided then and there that he would be her safe harbour. He would not muddy his mission with feelings, or want, or anything that could jeopardise that. For however long she needed it.

Petra wiped a hand over the mirror, clearing a smear of condensation.

Baby curls had sprung up around her face, her eyes dark with smudged mascara. She turned her head to the side and a whole-body shiver rocked through her as she remembered the feel of his mouth on her neck, the murmur of his voice, the slide of his tongue, leaving stubble rash on her neck.

If anyone doubted their story, that'd clinch it!

Laugh-crying—her new go-to mood—she let her head go till her forehead hit the mirror.

How had all that sprung from a conversation about *boundaries*? If she'd known that was all it would take, she'd have brought them up years ago!

Petra lifted her head away from the mirror. "What now?" she asked her reflection.

Did they take the boat back to the marina, walk hand in hand to her work, or his, smile at any photographers who tracked them down? Say, *Surprise! We're engaged!*

Maybe. Maybe not. First, she had to leave the bathroom.

Moving to the door, she pressed her ear against the wood and listened. What was Sawyer thinking out there? Was he still in the bed where she'd left him, splayed out, his big buff body covered in half a sheet? Or was he up and dressed and just going about his business as if all that was totally normal?

For the first time in her life, calling her mother felt like the easier option.

After all the messages her mother had left that morning, it went to voicemail. Of course, it did.

"Hey, Ma, it's Petra." Well, duh. "Just in case Deena's aunt has yet to fill you in, I wanted to tell you myself that Sawyer Mahoney and I are engaged! Woo-hoo!"

Woo-hoo? She squeezed her eyes shut.

"That night we reconnected, well, it turns out there *was* a spark. And always had been. For both of us."

Gosh, she hoped Sawyer couldn't hear any of this through the door.

"I didn't tell you before, because, as you can imagine, people are pretty interested in Sawyer's life and we wanted to keep it private, for just us, as long as we could. And quiet, so as not to overshadow things, such as my super-important work at the gallery. But alas. We could not hold back that tide."

She looked to the ceiling.

"I also didn't want to upset you. Considering his connection to Finn. Because of that, this wasn't an easy thing, for either of us. It took a lot for us both to get to this point. Just so you know."

A deep breath in and out.

"Anyhoo… The secret is out. Yay us. And yay to *no whiff of scandal*! And I won't let it get in the way of my work. So. That's it. Okay, 'bye."

Tossing her phone to the bench before she made it any worse, Petra wrapped the towel tighter around herself, took a deep breath and left the bathroom.

To find Sawyer was sitting on the edge of the bed, naked, the top sheet draped over his hips. The bed in which they'd just spent the last couple of hours. Or weeks. Who could be sure? They'd certainly left no stone unturned.

Sawyer lifted his head, his expression inscrutable as he took in the small towel, the messy bun atop her head, her face scrubbed clean.

She shrugged. *This is me.*

And when he smiled, breathing out hard as he slowly shook his head, as if he'd never found her more lovely, the emotions that swept over her were like nothing she'd ever felt before.

"So," she said. "That happened."

"Mmm… Do you reckon your princess and your carpenter would be proud?"

"Ha! I think they'd be blushing to their little PG cotton socks."

His smile was different. Easier somehow, lit with some new calm she'd never seen in him before.

When he asked, "You okay?" she didn't mind at all.

And this time she thought about her answer.

She'd imagined that being with him might get him out of her system, or take the edge off at least. Only that wasn't the case.

For the Sawyer she'd spent her life adoring was the Sawyer she'd built up in her head—the good, clean-cut, endearing, supportive, beautiful boy of her youth.

The Sawyer sitting before her, rumpled and scarred and tattooed, sparks of silver in his stubble, was complicated, and stubborn, and lonesome, and over-protective, and imperfect. Add to that the knowledge that he was also the most attentive lover imaginable. Generous, open and raw.

And what had once been a river of feeling that flowed through her was now all the oceans of the world.

"I am more than okay," she said.

"Glad to hear it." Then, gripping the sheet in one hand at his hip, he stood, looking like some

Roman god. He walked over to her, placed a finger under her chin, turned her head and winced. "I did that?"

"You did that."

She braced herself for an apology. But instead he smiled. No, he grinned. As if glad to have left his mark on her.

Then his gaze dropped, and the smile slipped away. Petra looked down to find her small towel had dropped open, revealing a sliver of skin down her right side. Her right thigh, the curve of her hip, the edge of her breast.

Sawyer's jaw clenched, his eyes glinting. Every muscle seeming to switch on, in the effort not to reach out and whip the thing away.

The last twenty-four hours had been a lot. The push and pull—all of it had come to a head, leading to them falling into bed.

But from here? From here it would be a choice. Whatever happened between them from this moment would redefine the parameters of their friendship for evermore.

It took her half a second's thought to let the towel fall. To move into his arms, press up onto her toes and kiss his jaw. His neck. The edge of his mouth.

It took him a little longer to make the same choice. But she got that. With Sawyer it always had.

He dropped the sheet and pulled her into his

arms, kissing her with a ferocity that turned her bones to mush.

"So," she said as he kissed his way down her neck. "Just so we're on the same page, when we go back out into the world, which we will have to do eventually—"

Sawyer cut her off with a growl. And a light kiss on the gravel rash that her had ovaries sighing.

"We are engaged."

"We are," he murmured, his mouth trailing along her shoulder and back to her earlobe.

"And neither of us has a problem being touchy-feely."

"Looks that way," he said, hands sliding down her back to cup her backside as he lifted her and carried her back to the bed where he sat, her knees settling each side of his hips. Where his gaze trailed over her body, his eyes dark and murky, like a man drunk on the view.

"And we are doing *this* now too," she managed to say, even while words and thoughts were becoming hard to find, as his mouth brushed back and forth over her collarbone.

"Seems so."

Then he lifted her and tossed her to the bed. Laughter shot from her lungs as she bounced, her hair splayed behind her head. Then her still damp skin brushed against his as he crawled his way up her body. Mouth brushing her belly, her breasts, before landing on her mouth, staking his claim.

As if he'd not staked it years before.

Then he made his way back down. Licking along her ribs, into her navel and pressing her legs apart, he made himself at home.

"Tell me," he said, his deep voice rumbling against her. "Tell me you want this."

"Yes," she said, pleasure already building inside her. Roiling like a wild thing.

"Tell me."

"I want this," she whispered. "I want you."

With the sense that he'd finally let himself off the leash, Sawyer licked her centre, before dragging her into his mouth.

Petra arced off the bed. Her nerves singing, her muscles aching. Her body still recovering from the past few hours. And yet she held on. Balanced on a knife-edge between too much and more *more*—

"More," she said, hardly recognising her own voice.

And he gave her more. He gave her everything she'd ever wanted.

But not for long.

Not for long.

For soon there was nothing left to want.

CHAPTER NINE

THE NEXT TWENTY-FOUR hours were a whirlwind. Starting with a quick trip to Sawyer's mum's place to tell her the news.

As Sawyer had suggested she might, Mrs Mahoney had given them both a pat on the cheek before showing off some of the grandkids' art on the fridge, her newfound priorities clear.

He'd then messaged Daisy on the way into Big Think. Her response was:

Punching above your weight much?

Then:

For Petra: He's a total pain. Good luck to you.

Hadley had made it clear they were to head into Big Think through the *front* door. "You're not rock stars," she'd apparently said. "Its past time you own this, so that the focus can shift back to where it belongs. On the work."

And she was right.

So, hand in hand, Petra and Sawyer passed another throng of 'reporters' shouting questions. This time they were asking when the big day would be, who'd be best man, and if Petra was knocked up.

Sawyer had talked to Petra the whole time, keeping her attention on him, his face, his smile, the protective glint in his eye, even while her heart had banged about in her throat.

Once inside the foyer of Big Think Tower, a grand three-storey atrium that took Petra's breath away, Sawyer had put his arm around her shoulders and pulled her close. While she'd taken the hand resting over her shoulder in her hand and held it tight.

Then upstairs, in an office she'd have picked as Sawyer's in an instant—considering the understated colours, the beautiful vintage map on the wall and the grand final medal draped over a bust of Groucho Marx—Hadley had sat them both down for "media training", to "get their stories straight".

While waiting for the hairdresser who was prepping them for their "candid engagement photo" to finish faffing with her fringe, Petra lifted her eyebrows at Sawyer, mouthing, *Does she know?*

Sawyer laughed. "That's just Hadley. Warm and fuzzy to her is like sunlight to a vampire."

"I heard that," said Hadley.

"Don't be mean," Petra said, smacking Sawyer on the arm by way of apology. "Hadley's put this all together for us with half a day's notice. She's a freaking queen."

Hadley had lifted her chin in agreement, while shooting Petra a quick smile. And in that moment Petra knew she'd made herself an ally.

Which had been quickly balanced out by her mother finally responding.

PASS ON OUR CONGRATULATIONS TO SAW-YER.

With an unexpected addendum:

AND DO TAKE CARE.

Then that afternoon, while working from the apartment, Mimi called to let her know the gallery management had been in touch to let her know they were fully on board with the Epic Dream Festival.

Mimi was over the moon when she relayed the phone call she'd received. "They said it sounds amazing! They can't wait to see what we come up with! Oh, and they sent congratulatory flowers as well, from the whole team. In fact, there are flowers everywhere in your office. From so many people. I hope you don't get hayfever."

Petra gave Mimi the required *rah-rah-rah*, while quietly noting they'd only found her idea exciting after Big Think had started leaking news of a possible announcement.

It was a relief to know she had a mandate going forward. One she could sink her teeth into. That was the point of the whole endeavour after all. But it was also deeply disquieting.

As Petra, the internationally renowned art curator, the gallery management had been unsure. Her boho clothes, her hand-drawn pitch making them look at her as if she wasn't worth their faith.

As Sawyer Mahoney's *fiancée* she was in like Flynn!

After spending a lifetime carving out her own space in the world, a space she'd had to work her ass off to make her own, once again a label she knew did not rightly belong to her defined her.

But the time she heard Sawyer's key in the apartment door lock she was pacing by the door, nibbling at her thumbnail, ready to vent.

Only the moment he opened the door and saw her there, waiting for him, he dropped his stuff to the floor, swept her up in his arms and had her up against the hallway wall before she could catch her breath.

And later, lying curled up against his side, her body humming with pleasure as she played with his hair, her head resting on his chest so that she could breathe in time with his heart, Petra decided not to bother him about it.

She'd made it pretty clear that she did not want

his help. Meaning she had to find her own way through the mental mire.

Which she could do just fine. She'd spent a lifetime doing just that, on her own, after all.

Hopping out of the taxi that dropped her to work the next morning, Petra saw the throng of photographers milling about the gallery entrance.

Determined to start as she meant to go on, and to claw back as much of her identity as she could before it was completely subsumed, Petra had insisted Sawyer head to his job, she to hers.

Armoured in her favourite swishy caramel velvet flares, a bottle-green top with a big soft bow at the neck, with teetering purple heels, she felt as ready as she could possibly feel as she headed towards the front doors.

"Petra!" called the first one, the rest perking up and racing her way.

"Over here!"

A camera flashed right in her eyes.

Sheesh.

"How did *you* land Mr Unlandable?" a reporter asked, a definite stress on the *you.* "Must be a hell of a prenup? What did you pop into his drink to get him to say yes?"

The others laughed. She knew that tone, having heard it in her parents' voices when she was really young. It was pure judgement.

As the way to the gallery seemed to lengthen

before her, Petra missed a step, her sharp heel teetering sideways for half a second before she found traction again. She hoped they couldn't see the pulse that had suddenly begun beating madly in her throat.

It hit her then. She was going about this all wrong. She was trying to do it *Sawyer's* way, not her own.

While he was all about protective armour, Petra was the human version of an exposed beating heart, her soft spots always on display for anyone to poke. She'd never faked it till she made it because she liked who she was, and relishing that had brought her more happiness than trying to please others ever had.

Which was why, chin up, shoulders squared, she spun on her heel and faced the throng. Like something out of a cartoon, their shoes squeaked on the concrete as they shot past her before circling back around.

Her heart still beat madly in her throat—because the whole thing was mighty intimidating—but of all the plans she'd made over the past few weeks, this one felt the most right.

"Hi." She waved. And waited till one of them waved back. "I'm Petra Gilpin. Assuming you're all here today because my fiancé…" still sounded weird "…is a public figure. While I'm not. So, I get why that makes you all a little curious. I hope it helps you understand why this—the swarming and the shouting—well, it's a lot!"

A couple of those nearest laughed, and her heart settled the tiniest bit.

"So, here's what I'm going to do," Petra said. "I'm giving you three answers to three questions. And that's it. So make 'em good."

One guy who looked like an old pro came on board fastest. "Where's the billion-dollar bling?"

Sawyer had offered. Petra had flat-out refused. It would be taking things a step too far. Or *another* step too far, at the very least.

"Just not a ring girl," she answered truthfully. She held up her hand and counted off. "That's one."

"Petra! Over here!"

She blinked into the waggling microphones and the wall of phones. For all that this felt better than the alternative, she wasn't sure how anyone got used to it.

"What's in the prenup?" a reporter at the back called.

"There isn't one."

Also true. Which felt better than *not denying*.

"But now you mention it, I feel a particular fondness for the Gilded Cage. Should I ask for that if it all goes pear-shaped?"

A smattering of laughter.

"Who've you signed with for the wedding photo exclusive?"

"I've been engaged for all of five minutes and

I can't leave the house without you lot there to say good morning. So, needless to say, any wedding questions will be answered with an *Um*..."

Much laughter at that one.

"The wedding exclusive- why do people do that?" she asked, genuinely interested.

"For the money," someone answered.

"Ah. Well, have you met my fiancé?" Laughter rolled through the group. And Petra felt such relief she was sure she was a foot taller. "Okay, well, that's three. Now, I have to get to work. So..."

She glanced back at the gallery, which looked lovely, all gothic and venerable in the early morning light. One guy lifted his camera and took a photo of the sign. She took that as a win! Petra gave them a wave and tried really hard not to run towards the doors.

She could have kissed Mimi, who met her there, sweeping her inside. While the photographers stopped, like a wave battering a beach, before subsiding back from whence they came.

"Wow," said Mimi, jogging beside her. "That was wild out there. But you were so cool. And I can't believe you're really engaged to Sawyer Mahoney. I mean, I can, because you're amazing, and he's amazing, but hot damn, Petra."

Mimi lifted her hand for a high five, which Petra duly returned.

"You're not secretly married, are you?" Mimi

asked out of the side of her mouth as they waited for the lift.

"What? No! Who's saying that?"

"People."

"What people?"

Mimi bit her lip, then said, "People on the internet. Or pregnant?" she whispered. "I know I'm not meant to ask, but just in case you get morning sickness I can be on alert."

After her win outside, Petra deflated. What if none of their efforts brought an end to the wrong kind of attention? What if no Barking Cat was born, and the heat didn't die down? What if everyone figured out it was fake, and the gallery was embroiled in yet another scandal, and her *actual* reputation ended up in tatters?

She had to get the Epic Dream Festival off the ground ASAP. There was no time to lose. Not only because it would make her parents look at her *differently*, but so that she could go back to looking at herself the same way she always had.

If she could sleep with Sawyer Mahoney, several times over, and not wake up to find he'd fled to Peru, then anything was possible.

"Are you ready to co-organise the biggest pop-up art collective this town has ever seen, have it marketed, ticketed and running in the next two weeks?"

Mimi blinked, then sat straighter in her chair. "What do you need me to do?"

Petra rattled off her ideas as they came to her. A stream of consciousness more than an actual plan. There were no wrong ideas—no wrong paths. Allowing the big, the bold, the wild, the wonderful some air made magic happen. And the more she spoke, the more she felt herself coming back into her own skin.

When Mimi left to get started, Petra called, "And lastly, set up lunch with Daisy Mahoney? I'll send you her number. She's stubborn, so do not take no for an answer."

"Consider it done."

Petra met Daisy for lunch. "It's happening."

"Really?"

Daisy bounced on her chair, looking like a kid again, hot pink tips and nose rings aside. "I have so many friends who are super keen. Can I send you their details?"

"Yes! Please! I'll make it my mission to check out each and every one asap. We need all hands on deck. Now and into the future. This is going to change the art scene in this town for ever."

"Wow. When you dream big, you dream big."

Petra breathed out and thought, *Hell, yes, I do.*

A notification buzzed on her wrist. A quick check of her phone found an article forwarded from Deena. The headline: *Art World Virtuoso Petra Gilpin and Big Think Partner Sawyer Mahoney Announce Engagement.*

It reeked of Hadley. Lots of lovely wholesome buzzwords, and Petra's name first, which she appreciated more than she could say.

Only the photo Hadley had gone with was not one of the media-friendly, smiling-into-the-distance shots they'd taken, it was a candid shot snapped when she was leaning into Sawyer, whispering into his ear.

Petra's hand was on Sawyer's knee, to get his attention. He was looking down at her, a small smile on his mouth, his eyes crinkled. They looked close, intimate, comfortable, and as if—

"Could there be any more goo-goo eyes and heart emojis?" said Daisy, half off her chair so she could gawp at Petra's phone.

Petra turned her phone face down on the table, having seen it too. And feeling more confused than ever as to what was real and what was not.

Daisy sat back. "Gross."

"Harsh!" Petra argued. "What's not to love about your big brother?"

"Plenty."

"Come on. He's a good guy. He'd do anything for you."

"Except stay."

Petra coughed on her drink, having to catch the dribble before it hit her shirt.

Daisy looked stricken. "I didn't mean he won't stay for *you*. I just mean he's away, a lot."

Petra smiled, even while she felt as if Daisy's

simple statement had hit a gong inside her. One that wouldn't stop chiming.

Ask her, and Petra would tell you Sawyer had always been there for her. But when she needed him *most*? The man carried the world on his shoulders. But when it came to intimacy, to putting down roots, to *love*, he was as reliable as a bucket with a hole in the bottom.

Which was when all the pieces of the puzzle seemed to slot together in her mind. Big Think wasn't his dream, but it had given him the chance to fall off the edge of the earth any time he needed to do just that.

"His work is important," Petra said. "As is mine. We'll figure it out. Now, lunch?"

It had been a long day at Big Think, starting with much the same treatment for Sawyer on his way into the tower.

"How'd a rogue like you land a lady like that? When's she due? Come on, mate, you'd think a guy in your position could afford to give her a damn ring!"

He found it far easier when such questions were targeted towards him. He did not feel near the same urge to take them by the scruff of the neck. And there had been another layer atop- the sense that he wanted to keep his answers private. As if it wasn't pretend.

He'd breathed easier once inside the lobby of Big

Think Tower, a spectacular monument to all that he and the boys had achieved in a mad few years.

The building was Ronan's dream, not his. Much like Big Think itself. But still, an incredible adventure to be a part of, something he'd never taken for granted. Also something he'd been thinking about, a lot, since Petra had made him consider his place there.

He'd taken his time walking through the lobby, noting how the soft sunlight fell through the three storeys of smoky glass windows, over an atrium filled with long leather couches and low tables, around which staff sat, drinking coffee and making plans. And he'd felt a wave of nostalgia come over him. As if he was looking back years from now.

Enough that he'd stopped to chat to everyone, checking what projects they were attached to, giving anyone who asked updates on the progress he'd made on his last trip. And accepting congratulations for his recent engagement.

By the time he'd even made it to the lift the expansive inlaid marble floor had done his leg no favours.

Nor had Petra climbing back into his bed that morning, bringing him a coffee—*"The one thing I can cook"*—before climbing on top and having her way with him. Totally worth it.

Now, back at the apartment, Sawyer searched for the video he was after and rolled out his leg on a foam cylinder, adapting the instructions on the screen to suit.

He could still remember the moment he'd broken his leg. *Catastrophic,* the commentators had called it. They'd put up a screen so that the crowd and cameras couldn't see, and even allowed an ambulance onto the field.

But he'd forgotten that he'd woken in the hospital with the strangest mix of emotions—fear that he might not walk again, and relief that one of the multitude of responsibilities he spent his life juggling had been taken from him. Till he'd felt the same sense of relief in asking Petra to marry him.

Fake or not, it didn't matter. What mattered was that, after butting heads about it for so long, she'd finally asked him for help. And it felt as if some deeply held truth had been unlocked inside him, leaving him free to let it be.

Near the end of the session, the front door rattled before it opened. The sound of Petra's bag hitting the floor, her shoes kicked off her feet, her keys landing somewhere on or near the hall table.

"Hey," he called, his voice strained, a yoga band wrapped around his big toe as he stretched out his hamstring.

Her face popped over the back of the couch. That lovely face. Soft hazel eyes, creamy skin, swishy auburn hair. All rumpled after what must have been a long day for her too.

"So, I saw you decided on an ad hoc press conference?"

She pulled a face. "I know, it just kind of happened. I tried to stick to your advice, but added a twist of my own. Hope that's okay?"

More than okay; she'd been phenomenal. Engaging, a little giddy, and utterly real. "Did it feel okay?"

"It felt…amazing." A nod, then she trailed her hand over the back of the couch as she rounded it, before she fell onto the thing and leaned up onto an elbow. "Now what are you doing?"

"*Pilates with Penny*," he grunted, motioning to the TV.

"I can see that," she said, her gaze flitting between his bare torso and the twenty-something American telling him to *"stretch, stretch, stretch…"*

He lifted up, his stomach muscles clenching as he found the remote and pressed pause. Liking the way her eyes widened as she stared.

"It's physical therapy," he said, falling back flat to the floor, sweat dripping down his cheek now that he'd stopped moving. "For my leg."

Petra's gaze roamed over his shoulders before moving over his ribs, then to his scars, plural, the result of multiple operations, running down the outside of his left leg, finishing just above his knee.

"Did we," she said, "hurt it…this morning? Or last night when I had you…"

"Backed up against a hard surface?" he finished, harking back to a particularly memorable conversation at the Gilded Cage.

She dropped her head to the couch, hands covering her face.

Sawyer laughed, letting his foot fall to the side so he could breathe. Then he heaved himself to sitting. Leaned an arm along the edge of the couch, his chin on the back of his hand.

Waiting for her to look at him.

Which she did, tipping her head sideways. Close enough he could see the myriad colours in her glorious eyes.

"Physical therapy is part of my life. You can't hurt me. I promise."

Her eyes moved from one of his to the other, wheels turning, before she asked, "When are you thinking about heading off again?"

Her voice was light, as if totally bored by her own question, proof to him it was anything but a throwaway line.

"No plans in place," he said. Which was true.

The fact that he'd spent most of the day thinking, seriously, *about* his next trip, he kept to himself. No point talking it over till he had something concrete to say.

"I'm going to finish stretching," he said, "then have a shower. You're welcome to watch."

Petra waved a hand his way. "Go ahead."

Lying back, he twisted his good knee to the

side, stretching out his glute. "I meant watch me in the shower."

She rolled her eyes before hauling herself to sitting. Then nibbled at her bottom lip, still thinking thoughts that put frown lines above her nose.

Sawyer distracted her with, "I'm going to the footy Saturday night. To shake hands with some Big Think big investors. Wanna be my date?"

Something flashed behind her eyes, wiping away her thoughts. Good. "You need a wingman?" she asked.

Dammit, she was incisive. Heading to the football was always a bit of a mind bend. Which, he was sure, it had to be for her too. "Think of it as a chance for us to take our engagement out for a spin."

"Okay, let's do it."

She gave his bare torso one last look, her gaze clouding with lust, before she hopped up and padded away. And it hit him how quickly things had changed. How openly she drank him in, when he used to catch the occasional telling flickers before.

It was hard not to imagine what it might be like living like this, living with her, for real. But that wasn't on the cards. He might be fake fiancé material but the rest was beyond him. He was busted, for one thing. Stretched too thin. And too used to not staying in one place too long.

She deserved better. She deserved the world.

In the shower, Sawyer turned the water scalding hot, letting the room fill with steam. A light knock had him lifting his head out from under the spray.

"Hello?"

Petra's voice came through the door, "I'm coming in."

No question. She opened the door and found her way through the mist. Her hair still a tumbled mess, only now she wore nothing but that same thoughtful expression.

He turned the water to a manageable heat, then opened the shower door and welcomed her inside.

And, without a word said between them, her hands glided up his chest as he moved back to let the water stream over her sleek skin. Pebbling her nipples. Gathering in pools at her décolletage.

His hands followed the streams, around her waist, over the curve of her bare backside.

She slid her hands over his shoulders, lifted up onto her toes and placed a kiss on his lips. Gentle. Intimate. So much so an ache hit right in the centre of his chest.

"How does your leg feel now?" she asked.

"What leg?" he said, and then he kissed her thoroughly. And made love to her against the shower wall with the dexterity of a man with four perfectly able limbs.

Making every hour he'd had to endure *Pilates with Penny* worth it.

CHAPTER TEN

SAWYER HAD TRAVERSED some of the most spectacular places on earth, but there was still nothing quite like looking out over the Melbourne Cricket Ground, the home of Australian Rules football—the grass a pristine green, the sky cerulean blue, the energy of the football crowd creating an electric storm in the air.

Watching Petra lean over the railing as she tried to count the rows of seats on the level below he did not love as much.

"Finn would have loved this," she said.

"The best seats in the house?" Sawyer reached out and hooked a finger through her belt loop, readying to haul her back if she tipped too far. "Hell, yeah, he would."

Then realised belatedly that they were talking about Finn and none of the usual heaviness settled on his shoulders. He felt more a phantom pain than immediate and raw.

She looked back at him when he added an extra finger. "You all right there?"

"Just can't keep my hands off you," he said.

She stilled. The way she had again and again

over the last few days as they'd settled into their new normal. As if waiting for the other shoe to drop. "Shouldn't you be saving that gold for when we have prying ears listening in?"

Sawyer gave her jeans a little tug. "Trying it out on a test audience first seems a smart move."

Petra spun about slowly, taking his hand with her till his arm was wrapped around her and he had her backed up against the railing. "What else you got?"

He leaned in, calling her bluff. Only for her scent to hit the back of his tongue—so sweet and warm and heady, making him forget what he'd been going to say. So he kissed her instead, sweeping his tongue into her mouth when she gasped.

When they pulled apart her eyes were dark, her cheeks pink. "Aren't we here to project a *wholesome* image?"

"You, Ms Gilpin, are here today to trawl the private room behind me for those with the deepest pockets, so that you can sweet-talk them into sponsoring one of your pop-ups."

She grinned. It was blinding. Literally. He felt his brain go blank for a second. Meaning he wasn't ready for her when she lifted onto her toes and nipped at his bottom lip.

Then she pulled back, ducked under his arm, grabbed his hand in hers and dragged him up the stairs towards the corporate box.

"Mahoney!"

Sawyer looked up to find a bunch of footy fans

decked out in black and white on the third level, waving. And filming. Petra looked up, smiled and waved. And they cheered.

Because since her "three questions and three answers" chat out in front of the gallery she'd become quite the hit. According to Hadley, *Have you met my fiancé?* was a trending meme on social media.

Petra looked back at him then, pink-cheeked, eyes filled with laughter. Heart-achingly beautiful. And he found himself wishing, hoping, that none of that had been for an audience. That it had all been for him.

The glass doors leading to the corporate box slid open and Sawyer spotted Hadley and Ronan.

Petra made her way straight to them, leaning in to kiss Hadley's cheek.

"Aren't you a dark horse," said Hadley, eyeing her sideways as if she was checking to see what other skills she might be hiding.

Petra made a *pffft* sound, brushing it off, before giving Ronan a big bear hug. Which he accepted with a grumble.

"Why are you wearing those colours?" Ronan asked.

Petra flapped her black and white scarf in his face. "Why aren't you? Sawyer *played* for Collingwood—you can't possibly go for anyone else."

Ronan tapped the small navy and red pin he wore on his dark suit lapel. Petra rolled her eyes.

"Of course, you go for Melbourne. You are such a cliché."

Sawyer moved to Hadley's side when it became clear the other two were happy to go toe-to-toe. "Checking up on me?"

Hadley brought a glass of wine to her lips. "I'm here to watch the players. I like their short shorts."

"I still have mine, if you'd like to borrow them—?"

"No," said Hadley, shivering from head to toe. "You've done your time, for now. So, I found you a trip. Wanna go to the Northern Territory for a couple of days?"

He opened his mouth to say *Hell, yes*. For he'd been nudging Hadley for the chance since telling Petra about the clinic he'd started up there, in his pre-Big Think days. Only now he had someone else to consider.

"Hey, Petra." He whistled to get her attention. "You okay for me to go to Darwin for a couple of days?"

Hadley coughed on her drink. Then made a whip cracking sound.

Sawyer, ignoring her, waited for Petra to blink. And say, "Oh. Ah…sure. Of course."

"Yep," he said to Hadley, "I can go to Darwin." Then, with a waggle of his eyebrows, he moved to Petra's side as Ronan asked, "How'd you get roped into trying to save the gallery, that old dinosaur?"

"I'm an altruist."

Ronan snorted. "It's on its last legs, from what

I hear. Be my conduit, help me buy the gallery building. I'll give it to Ted for more lab space."

"Care to sponsor a pop-up modern art collection instead?" Petra asked. "Give me enough money and I can name a gallery wing after you." She held out a hand as if writing the name across the sky. "The Ronan Gerard Experience."

"That's all we need," Hadley muttered, then lost interest, ambling off to find another drink. Ronan followed.

"So, Darwin," Petra said. "Just a couple of days?"

"Just a couple of days."

"You could check on the rehab clinic!"

His smile came from some deep place inside him, loosening everything in its path. "I certainly could. Now, come with me. I see some Melbourne supporters who look in need of some wallet-lightening."

The Magpies won in a thriller, with a goal after the siren.

Add the several enthusiastic contacts Petra had made, who were keen to talk more about her pop-up collection sponsorship plan, as well as pick her brain about their private art collections, and Petra could not have had a better night.

But it was the Darwin thing that had her feeling as if she were floating an inch off the ground.

Sawyer was going away. Only this time he'd let her know. And she couldn't help but feel as if they had turned some corner in their relationship. As if it might, maybe, truly be leading to something real.

Once home, while Sawyer was getting a drink, Petra checked her messages to find one from her mother.

Squinting with one eye, she read it.

YOUR FATHER SAW THE PHOTO OF THE TWO OF YOU ONLINE. STILL AS HANDSOME AS THE DEVIL, THAT ONE...

Petra's eyes opened wide as she coughed out a laugh. No passive aggression. No dig. If not for the capital letters, she'd wonder if she was being catfished by someone pretending to be her mother.

She replied:

My father? Or Sawyer?

FUNNY GIRL.

Petra smiled, and popped her phone on the small dining table, spun on her heel and reached for her talisman, her necklace with the engagement pull tab attached, only to find it wasn't there.

"What's wrong?" Sawyer asked as he set a pot on the stove.

"I can't find my necklace. The rose gold one. The one with the... The one Finn gave me."

Sawyer stopped what he was doing, ready to spring into action. And while that side of him had always frustrated her, now she found it endearing.

"Were you wearing it today?" he asked.

"I wear it *always*. I was definitely playing with it, in the game's dying minutes."

Her scarf! She plucked it from the floor pile and gave it a shake. Only for the necklace to fling free and land with a delicate slump.

Sawyer picked it up, the thin chain so small in his big hand. The aluminium pull tab he'd offered up as an engagement ring, twice, a clunky dented silver thing glinting up at him.

She watched him run his thumb over the silver circle, his expression unreadable. Then he bounced it up and down on his hand, the chain dragging lightly behind, before his gaze swept to hers, full of questions. Most likely regarding why she wore a fake engagement doodad so close to her heart.

But Petra was deep inside a memory of her eighteenth birthday party. The pull tab from his beer. Bouncing the thing up and down as she'd played a silly game about who she would one day marry.

Was that *why* he'd chosen it that night at the club? Because it had meaning for them? For him?

She walked to him on shaky legs. Placed her hand over his, trapping the necklace and the "ring", their torrid history, the push and pull of their story, right there, between their palms.

And waited for him to look up.

"That night," she said, feeling brave and terrified all at once, "at my party, when I was bouncing the pull tab on my hand, I was trying to stop at the letter S."

His throat worked, as if fighting against what she was trying to tell him.

"I had such a crush on you back then."

Sawyer's chest rose, his brow tight, as he said, "I knew."

"You *did*?"

"You wore your heart on your sleeve back then. Just right out there. Fearlessly. Everyone else I knew, Finn included, hid behind charm, or politeness, or fear. But you…you were so wholly yourself. You were mesmerising."

"And now?" she asked, feeling breathless. Hollow.

"Can't read you quite so well," he said, his eyes now searching hers. "But the mesmerising thing still stands."

With that, she took the necklace from his hand, lifted it till the pull tab dangled between them. A big shiny sign of how she'd once felt about him. How she felt about him still.

He motioned for her to turn around, lifted her hair off her neck and fixed the clasp. Then he kissed her, the clasp between his lips and her skin, before letting her hair drop back into place.

"When do you leave?" she asked, knowing she'd miss having him near. But so staggered he'd let her know. Not that it negated Daisy's point, that he *couldn't* stay. But it was something. She was *sure* it meant something good.

"Tomorrow morning," he said. "If that suits you."

She nodded. "Then we'd better not waste any more time."

Petra took him by the hand and led him into her bedroom.

Her clothes were messily draped over the end of her bed. A jacket and a bra over the back of a padded chair. And a small cut-crystal bowl with a pink stone, a pink button, pink chalk and a pink feather had pride of place on her chest of drawers.

She gave Sawyer a small shove and he dutifully lay back on her bed, watching as she slowly took off every item of clothing, bar the necklace carrying his ring.

Then, as if he knew that she needed this, that she felt strong and brave, he let her divest him of his clothes too.

Planning to take her sweet time, she worked her way up his body, touching, stroking, caressing, nipping where she saw fit, before she lay along his side, her leg hooked over his, as she traced the massive phoenix tattoo curling over Sawyer's shoulder. "When did you get this one?"

He lifted his chin and watched her finger. "Started it the week I walked on my own for the first time after I broke my leg. Took several sessions. And a few touch-ups."

"Did it hurt?"

"Like a son of a bitch."

Knowing him, she imagined the pain was part of the reason why. "And yet you got more. Tell me about them. I want to know them all."

He lifted a little, pulling at his tight skin to show a mountain scene. "I got this one in a little hole in the wall in Mexico City last year. It was the most gorgeous place I'd seen in some while. I found a hospital full of kids with limb injuries. Burns. All in need of rehab. It felt as if I'd come full circle."

"You light up when you talk about that, you know? The rehab." Lit up and lightened up. "It could be something you turn your focus to, if you ever lose the will to sleep on jungle floors."

She felt his chest rise and fall under her hand. Then under her mouth as she kissed her way over the mountains. Running her tongue along its ragged edges.

She knew she could have talked more about her idea. Her certainty that he'd find real purpose in that kind of work. But Sawyer was not a man to be told. He had to figure it out for himself. So she kissed her way over the ocean waves, the spring flowers, the AFL football, the magpie, the date of the grand final he'd won his first year. This map of the life he'd lived without her.

Only to stop short when she saw the single feather floating over his left pec. It was tiny, delicate, pink, with a watercolour finish. It looked ethereal, magical, the only tattoo that wasn't pure black.

It was her.

His eyes lifted to hers and he knew what she'd found.

The urge to ask him about it, to know how long he'd had it, for him to tell her why, was so strong her throat burned with the need to ask.

But she could feel the rubber band holding him back. The same one he'd used to keep himself in one piece while everyone in his life pulled him in a thousand different directions, knowing he was strong enough not to break.

Petra didn't want to be something he had to navigate. She wanted to be the one he came home to when he was done.

So she kissed him, and held him, and sighed as he did the same to her.

Then he reached towards her bedroom drawer, in search of another condom.

"Wait!" she cried.

"What?"

"Not that drawer."

"What's in that drawer?"

She bit her lip so as not to say.

A smile spread across Sawyer's face as he figured it out. "Now I have to open that drawer."

"Why?"

"I want to meet the competition."

"Russell's not your competition."

"Oh, I know that," he said, shooting her a look that made her blush all over. "I'm his."

Laughing despite herself, she waved a hand to her bedside drawer. Eyes closed, biting her lip as Sawyer slowly opened it with grave ceremony, only stopping when he found the man of the hour.

"Good God," he said, pulling out her big, bold, bright purple vibrator with its cute bunny ears.

Petra's hands flew to her face.

"Oh, *now* you're hiding. You brought him up easily enough that night at the club. Russell this and Russell that. Mind you, he's impressive as hell."

She laughed and wriggled till she had the sheet over her head.

Then she heard the tell-tale buzz. Russell was turned on.

The sheet was tugged gently before Sawyer whipped it away, leaving her bare. Laughing, she held up her hands to push him away.

He waited for her to calm down before lowering the vibrator till it hovered, buzzing just above her belly, "May I?"

His eyes were dark, his jaw tight. That face, that beautiful face, wanted her. And while she now knew that he knew she'd wanted him for ever, she'd take it. Whatever she could have of him.

She nodded. Then, "First, are you sure you know how to wield that thing?"

"I'm an athlete," he said, "I learn quick."

And boy, did he.

* * *

A few days later, longer than he'd intended, Sawyer stood beneath the large covered porch area annexe outside Petra's apartment building, collar turned up against the chill and the rain now coming down so hard it was near sideways.

Enough to keep away any press.

Or maybe they'd given up on him and moved completely to team Petra.

There was the chance that their ruse had worked. With no new nightclub vision coming out, just a well-written announcement and Petra's openness, it was possible they were no longer of interest.

It was also possible that the fact that he'd not been around had given Petra a reprieve. Which, if true, needed consideration.

Then again, a barking cat *might* have been born and the press were merely distracted. Better leave things as they were till he found out for sure.

Now, where the heck was Petra?

He was itching to tell her about the rehab centre. The feeling of rightness that had come over him the minute he'd set foot in the place. The ideas that had unspooled.

And to see her, hold her, maybe even wrap her up in his coat and not let her go.

She wasn't at the gallery. He'd called. Their closing hour had long since passed. She wasn't home, in their apartment. Her apartment? *The* apartment. And she wasn't answering her mobile.

In fact, she'd been mighty hard to get onto the whole time he was away, having apparently gone into hyper-focus mode, working crazy long days the way he knew she usually did when she was in the midst of a project she really loved.

Meaning everything must have been going brilliantly in his absence.

Another thing to consider that, it turned out, he wasn't in the mood to consider.

Not until he saw her. Held her. Kissed her. Told her that she was absolutely right and that it turned out he was, in fact, a man with a dream.

Till then he stamped his feet to ward off the cold and tried not to imagine other places she might be. Such as stuck in a lift somewhere. Or lost down a well. How long *had* it been since he'd last heard from her? Eighteen hours? Twenty-four? He checked his battered watch. It was after nine at night. Late home for her.

He found himself remembering the times Daisy used to run away, as a kid. The times his mother would call, her voice slurred, and he'd drive home, imagining the worst, only to find she'd had a glass of Baileys on an empty stomach. Then there'd been the phone call telling him Finn had broken his neck.

He looked to his phone. Who could he call, just to ease his mind?

There was only one.

He called Petra's mother.

"Dr Gilpin," she answered in her clipped tone.

"Josephine, it's Sawyer. Sawyer Mahoney."

A beat, then, "Well. Hello."

Sawyer swore at the sky, wishing he'd not been so rash, but he was there now. "Sorry to call so late, but I was wondering if you've heard from Petra in the last day or so."

"No, not in that time-frame. Why? Has she meandered off somewhere? She used to do that a lot, as a child. If you're really going to marry her, do keep that in mind."

Sawyer's jaw ached from not throwing back, *Of course I'm going to marry her.* But he didn't want to make things more complicated for Petra with her parents than they already were. "I've been away, and now I'm back and she's not home, and… And I sound like a fool."

Josephine laughed, the sound so like her daughter. "Not at all. I remember what it was like those first years Josiah and I were together. Young love can be quite the rush. Don't worry. She'll find you when she's ready. She always worked on her own timeline that one."

It surprised him to find a note of affection in Josephine's voice, considering what he knew of how they'd interacted when Petra was younger. And Petra's continued lack of faith in her parents' affections.

It surprised him and gave him great relief. To know that he had support in supporting her.

"You're right," he said, his voice a little rough. "I should let you go."

"Not at all, it was lovely to hear from you, Sawyer. It's been a while." Then, "It's *his* birthday soon, you know."

Sawyer nodded. "I know. Petra keeps trying to nudge me to do something with her to celebrate. Has she done the same with you?"

"She has at that, but I fear I've not been as receptive as she might have hoped."

"She'll give you another chance," he said.

"Full of infinite chances, that one," said Josephine.

The memory of Finn – stubborn and restless, compared with Petra and her wide open heart– wavered between them before it fluttered away.

"As for my younger child," said Josephine, as if she'd read Sawyer's mind, "while she might appear as if she's far stronger than us all, her tender side is stronger still. Do remember that."

With that, Josephine Gilpin rang off, leaving Sawyer feeling as if a weight that had been on his shoulders all these years had been lifted.

Pocketing his phone, he looked down the street and—

There. Petra. Walking up the footpath.

Rain was now pelting down, but she didn't even seem to notice. In fact, she tilted her face to the water and soaked it in. Her hair was dark red as it stuck to her cheeks and neck. Her boots splashing through puddles.

Only Petra, he thought, his chest tightening at the sight of her, as if he missed her more now that she was so close. *Only her.*

"Petra! What the hell are you doing out here?" he called when she was close enough to hear him, stepping out into the rain as he waved his arm in the air.

Petra stopped when she heard her name. Grinned when she saw him. Then ran into his arms.

He lifted her, twirling her about on the spot till the rain ran down his face, down the back of his shirt, into his shoes. When she slid down his body she kissed him. Hard.

"You're back!" she said, as if slightly surprised.

"That I am," he said.

"And no press?" she said, glancing around.

"Seems they've grown weary of us."

"Oh, I doubt that. A magazine called me today, asking if I could do three questions and three answers for their online stream."

"Wow, that's… You tell me?"

"I said only so long as it was about my work. They're yet to get back to me." She smiled from ear to ear. "Today was a good day. I wanted it to last as long as possible. So I walked home. And then it started to rain. And here I am!"

"What was so good about today?" he asked.

"The Epic Dream Festival is good to go. We

bump in from tomorrow, and it begins over the weekend. Despite evidence to the contrary, the weather is going to be perfect!"

"It wouldn't dare be otherwise."

"Right? Then Mimi, the wonder that she is, started a whisper campaign. And everyone is talking about it. Including major sponsors, which brought in more artists willing to do pop-ups. Which are now booked for months to come!"

"That's incredible."

"And then I hear my favourite gallery in New York is looking for a guest curator for their autumn season. And Daisy put me onto this fantastic underground German art club that I'm dying to check out. It's as if the universe knew I was missing you and did everything possible to make me feel better."

Sawyer smiled, even while his brain was suffering from an overload of information.

She missed him. She was making plans, far-away plans, for the not-too-distant future. She'd nearly done what she'd come home to do.

He'd gone to the Northern Territory to reconnect with his past. Only, instead, to find himself seeing a future. Not a future spent living for someone else, but one he wanted for himself. One which Petra could be part of.

Only now, seeing how happy she looked at the thought of doing what she'd set out to do, which was to help the gallery get back on its feet, before heading back to her amazing real life, he realised how selfish that would be.

Right as he was ready to put down roots for the first time in his adult life, his reason why was just learning to fly.

"How about you?" she asked, flicking water from her eyes. "Anyone at the rehab centre who remembered you? Was it hot up there? Did you eat crocodile?"

"I'll tell you all about it later. But first..." He lifted her bodily and walked her out of the rain. And there, beneath the bright light of the annexe, he kissed her.

He kissed her as they made their way up in the lift. Kissed her as they tumbled through her apartment door. Kissed her as they struggled to tear the wet clothes from one another's bodies.

Then lifted her into his arms and carried her to his bed. Where they made love. There was no other way to describe it.

And later, as she lay snoring softly in his arms, he told himself he'd find the right time to tell her about his plans later. Even while he knew that version of later was already nothing but a dream.

The night before the Epic Dream Festival was set to launch, the gang were having a night. The six of them—Adelaid and Ted, Sawyer and Petra, Ronan and Hadley—enjoying mouth-wateringly good bubbly and deliriously delicious antipasto on the gorgeously appointed balcony taking up a good portion of Ronan's floor of the Big Think Tower.

Petra leant on the heavy concrete balustrade, looking out over the river. For Melbourne had really put on a show. A crystal-clear night, stars peppering the inky black above, the city set to let off fireworks due to some other festival Petra hadn't quite caught the name of.

Though they were all there to celebrate *her* success. Apparently Big Think was big on that kind of thing. And, it seemed, since she was with Sawyer, they considered her part of the family too.

While Petra finally felt as if she'd found herself again. She felt as if she was truly living inside her own skin.

Petra turned to see Ronan holding what looked like a small cactus that Adelaid had presented him with on arrival. Ted was holding up his hands, as if miming *Don't blame me!*

Hadley was refilling everyone's drinks, while Sawyer poured chips into a big bowl. He'd ditched his jacket, and the edges of his tattoos caught the light. He looked so big, and strong, and grounded.

It hit her in that moment, with the gentle grace of an autumn leaf fluttering to the ground, that she had fallen in love with him.

Not the crush she'd had as a kid. Or the hots she'd felt as a teen. But love. Big, sweeping, scary, raw love.

She had to tell him. And she would. When the

time was right. For things were still new, and precious, all the pieces holding them together stacked like a house of cards.

Once she got through the first day of the festival, and went home, and crawled into his bed, exhausted and happy and spent, she'd tell him then. Maybe.

Hadley came over and gave her a glass. "I can't even look at you."

"What's that, now?"

"The way you are gazing at that lug of a man. I'll need a fire extinguisher by the end of the night."

Petra laughed, but didn't deny it.

"You guys have some fantastical goodbye night planned?" Adelaid asked as she joined them.

Caught watching Adelaid suck up a whole glass of iced water in one go—pregnant with baby number two, apparently cold water was her thing—Petra had to rewind to replay what she'd said.

"Who's saying goodbye?" Petra asked.

Adelaid looked to Hadley, then across to Sawyer, then back again.

Hadley, not one to pull her punches, said, "Sawyer. Thought we'd have him a bit longer this time, considering. But he's off again next week. A month or more, much of it completely off-grid. Prepare yourself- as for Sawyer, this usually means another three months of him faffing about the place, spending the company money on any hard luck story he finds."

"Hadley…" Adelaid chastised, and Petra realised she must look as pale as she suddenly felt.

One time he'd given her a heads-up, and she'd believed he was no longer beholden to whatever used to make him disappear in the first place.

Instead, while she'd been standing there feeling smug about how well she had a handle on things, so much she'd admitted to herself that she loved the guy, Sawyer was making plans to leave. As if their dalliance was a blip on his timeline. As if, when it came down to it, she wasn't enough for him to change his plans. His ways. His heart.

"Excuse me," she said, pressing away from the railing, her body feeling as if it had been wrapped in cotton wool.

Sawyer looked up, his gaze tracking her, as if he had some kind of radar where she was concerned.

Pressing back the very real urge to cry, Petra cocked her head, beckoning him to meet her inside, then walked through the French windows and into Ronan's kitchen.

"Hey," Sawyer said as he joined her. "Everything okay?"

Petra moved around the other side of the bench, out of his reach, not trusting herself not to lean on him, hold him, kiss him in the hope it would break whatever spell meant he couldn't love her the way she loved him.

"So," she said, her voice thick. "I had a thought."

He mirrored her stance and said, "Hit me with it."

"What with the Festival happening tomorrow, I've done what I came here to do. I think this would be a great time for us to...tear off the Band-Aid."

"What Band-Aid?"

"The fake engagement Band-Aid."

Petra saw the moment he realised what she meant. Agony seemed to sweep across his beautiful blue eyes, before the shutters came slamming down.

"You want to do this here?" he asked, his tone crisp and cool. "Now?"

"I think it's best," she lied. Needing it over, before she fell in a heap. "I've had a few feelers come my way—"

"So you said," he shot back, his voice raw.

She had? She didn't remember that. Had *that* played into *his* reason for making plans to leave? Because he thought that was *her* plan? Surely not.

"This was always temporary, Sawyer. A means to an end. And what with your plans to leave next week, the time seems right—"

"What plans?" he said, moving towards her, his expression fierce.

"Hadley mentioned you are going away again. For months. Actually, Adelaid mentioned it first, then Hadley confirmed." Leaving her, as always, the last to know. "While I *did* ask that you give me a heads-up if you made such plans, as it happens your timing is perfect."

His jaw worked so hard she feared he might

break a tooth. And a huge part of her hoped that he might fight back. That he might tell her that she was mistaken, that he wasn't going anywhere. That it had never been a ruse. Not for him.

Instead he said, "What do you need me to do?"

Love me back! she thought. And very nearly said it.

Till he said, "Do you need me to go with you and tell them we're over?"

Them? Petra risked a look over Sawyer's shoulder to find the other four had gathered at the far end of the balcony, giving them privacy. As if they already knew what was coming.

Deflating—like an unexpectedly pricked balloon—she figured they'd probably expected it of Sawyer from day one. How mortifying to know she was the only one left surprised.

"You can tell them whatever you like. They're your people."

People she'd come to really like, which was a big thing for her. And now she was losing them too.

She shook her head. "I'm going. I have a huge day tomorrow anyway. And I think it's best you don't come home tonight. It might seem…confusing, to anyone paying attention. Perhaps you could head back to the Elysium till you go. Then we tie our story off with a neat bow."

Sawyer ran both hands over his face, and through his hair, finishing with them gripping the back of his neck. He looked…confused. No, he looked harrowed. And yet he still said, "Okay. If that's what you want."

It's not what I want! a voice screamed in the back of her head. How she kept it there she had no idea. Some last, wobbly thread of self-protection held her together while her insides were shaking apart.

He'd been too good a friend for this to end so badly. So she walked around the bench, put her hand on his chest, right over the pink feather tattoo, and leaned in to press a kiss to his cheek. Closing her eyes, committing to memory the roughness of his skin, his warmth, his strength. As if it wasn't already indelibly marked on her psyche.

When he sucked in a long slow breath she imagined he was doing the same.

But what did it matter? What could she do? Beg him to make another promise he didn't mean?

If *his* issues meant he was afraid to commit, unwilling to change, unable to love her then she was done hoping. Done waiting. She was not going to live the emotional roller coaster of loving him. Not any more.

"Thank you," she said, pulling back and looking him in the eye.

"For what?"

"For putting those pretending skills of yours to good use. I was floundering, and you saved me. Which was all *you* ever wanted."

His jaw clenched. His eyes searched hers. But she didn't want him to see inside her, not any more.

"You know what the funniest thing about all this has been. Finn would have loved seeing us together. But even if he hadn't, it would not have been his choice."

"Petra," Sawyer said, his voice ragged, finally showing emotion, his expression pained.

But she was done. Spent. Wrung out.

If being with him had taught her anything- and after having to put up with the push and pull of her parents' affections her entire childhood- it was that her feelings were valuable. Worthy. That she did not have to accept anything less than whatever it was she wanted.

And if he couldn't give it to her, then it was out of her hands.

"Goodbye, Sawyer," she said. "I hope you find what you're looking for out there."

Then, without looking back, she turned and walked away.

CHAPTER ELEVEN

"AREN'T YOU GONE YET?" Hadley stood in the doorway to the Big Think Founders' Room—which looked more like a university den—glaring at Sawyer as he tried to come in.

"Trying to," he growled, not in the mood for her attitude. "One last meeting then I'm out of here. So please move out of my way, or I will physically move you."

"I'd like to see you try," Ronan's voice called from inside the room. "Get in here."

Sawyer pressed past Hadley, who moved her foot at the last moment, as if about to trip him.

"Seriously?" he barked.

She curled her lip and let him by.

"What's your problem?" Ronan asked.

Sawyer took off his jacket and tossed it over the back of a chair, then sat astride the seat. "My leg," he lied, rubbing the offending spot.

"His leg is *not* his problem," said Ted, while pulling apart a mobile phone and putting it back together again. "That would be Petra. She did not go home with a headache last night. He did something to screw it all up."

Sawyer hadn't told them, in the end, that things were over. He'd made his excuses and left himself soon after, heading to the boat, where he'd slept on sheets that still smelled like her. Because he couldn't believe it himself. In his eyes, in his plans, they were only at the beginning.

"I did not screw anything up. I—" How could he put it without giving Petra away? "I need to take this trip. Check up on those I've helped set up in the past, and hand them over to their new contacts so that I can start my new project."

Ronan picked up a piece of paper he had at hand and read, "The Big Think Centres for Physical Therapy."

"That's the one. I want to start by refurbishing a centre in Darwin. And building a few other rural centres, in consultation with the communities up there."

He waited for Ronan to shut him down. To say it was too narrow a focus. If he did, then Sawyer was ready to walk. Go at it on his own. It felt that important to him. That right. And right now it was the only thing that *did* feel right.

But Ronan only nodded. "Does Petra have something against rehab?"

"She wasn't upset because Sawyer's going, she's upset he didn't tell her he was going," said Ted. Then, noticing the surprised silence that came on top of his rare emotional insight, he added, "At least that's what Adelaid thinks."

"Why the hell didn't you tell her?" Ronan asked.

Because he was only just getting his head around the fact that he could do something for himself. As soon as he told her, she'd know it was because of her. She'd know how much of an impact she made on him. And he might as well prise open his ribs, point to his heart and say, *There, take it, it's yours.*

Complete and utter capitulation, which would negate all the work he'd done to be her support system above all else.

"Harking back to Hadley's earlier point," said Sawyer, attempting to distract them into getting on with the damn meeting so he could get the hell out of there. "I'm leaving asap. So can we get on with the meeting so I can tie up any loose ends before I go?"

"What about Petra?" Ted, Ronan and Hadley spoke at the same time.

Sawyer let his face fall into his hands. Then rubbed it. Hard. He might even have growled before taking the chance to glare at each one of them. "Leave Petra out of this."

"After you," said Ted.

Sawyer glanced Ted's way. "When did you become the foremost expert on...all this?"

"Since I fell in love," said Ted, with not even a hint of irony.

Once again Sawyer looked at the others, intimating, *Can you believe this guy?*

But they were all three looking at him as if *he* needed help.

"You're an idiot," said Hadley, clearly loving this.

While Ronan sat back in his throne, making it clear he was in this now. They were not moving on until the subject was resolved. "Usually I'd be all for you having no life outside of Big Think—you know that, right?"

Sawyer was well aware.

"But the terrible truth is, we are also allowed to live lives outside of this building. This job."

"You don't," Sawyer shot back.

Hadley cleared her throat. Was that a flush rising up her neck when everyone looked her way? "What? I breathed the wrong way."

Ronan looked at her for a long moment before turning back to Sawyer.

"Either way, we are all in agreement. Only a fool would let Petra go."

"I honestly can't believe that this is the room in which decisions are made regarding billions of dollars' worth of funding. And all you want to do is talk about my love life?"

"He loves her." That was Hadley. "I *knew* it."

Then, in a last-ditch effort to put this thing to bed, Sawyer found himself saying, "It was fake!"

"What do you mean, fake?" Ronan asked.

Sawyer knew he could trust the people in this room. With his life. He'd already done so for years. Still, it took him a few beats longer to feel sure he could trust them with Petra's.

"The thing with Petra. It wasn't real."

He went on to explain. "That scene in the club, it was a kind of in joke gone wrong. When the video came out, she didn't need the negative press that would come with a denial so we rolled with it. Then, when the time seemed appropriate, we 'broke up'."

He added air quotes. Though they were half-hearted. Every move he'd made since that night at Ronan's had felt half-hearted. As if when she'd left she'd taken a big part of him with her. The part of him that had always been hers.

He blinked to find them all watching him. No humour, no reproof, just...pity.

Sawyer pushed himself to standing, grabbed his jacket and began to slide his arms through the holes.

"You love her," Hadley said, matter-of-fact.

"Of course I bloody love her!"

Sawyer's words echoed around the room, inside his head, his heart. And he sat back down, his jacket half on, half off.

He loved her. He was in love with Petra. Madly, completely, insanely. To the point that he couldn't see straight where she was concerned, and never had.

"Then go get her," Ronan said.

Go get her. As if it was that simple.

Only, wasn't it?

She'd asked him once to trust her. Trust her to make her own choices, make her own mistakes. If he didn't tell her how he felt, explain why he'd made the choices he had, then he'd be denying her that.

And he didn't want to deny her anything.

Sawyer shot out of the chair, into the lift, through the lobby and outside. Onto the street. Where he pulled out his battered old phone and pulled up Petra's number.

What to tell her?

That he finally knew what he wanted? Finally knew where his passions lay?

On the couch with her, her feet on his lap as she melted over nineties French cinema. Following her down garden paths, his shirt scooped ready to carry anything she found. Tucked up beside her in bed, even when her feet were cold.

Imagining the real possibility of that life being his for ever, he made the call.

She'd done it. Petra had done what she'd set out to do.

The Epic Dream Festival had taken over the forecourt of the Gallery of Melbourne, transforming the space into a maze of wonder and delight. From the fairy floss stands to the beautiful vintage merry-go-round that pealed haunting music up into the sky, the pale pink velvet ropes herding people past pop-up stands filled with the most eclectic to the new façade of the gallery itself, it was nothing short of wondrous.

It wasn't exactly within the purview that she'd been given, but the gallery was back on the map, had money in the bank, and Petra had done it her way.

While the press, in the end, had been a boon. The memes, as well as the rapport she'd built with the regulars who followed her, three questions ready to go every day, had shone an unexpected light over her plight.

And the people had come, as she'd absolutely known they would. They'd bought tickets, and food, and pieces from the amazing, prolific young artists who'd rallied to her cry.

And even while her eyes felt gritty and small behind her big dark sunglasses, even while her heart felt like a shrivelled-up prune, and even while her parents still might not understand her approach, she felt proud of what she'd achieved.

It was called multi-tasking.

"This is amazing!"

Dredging up a smile, Petra glanced over at Deena, who'd stopped in front of a life-sized nude sculpture with a chocolate wrapper in place of a fig leaf.

"Put in a bid." Petra nudged her. "Think of it as a tax deductible talking point for your firm."

Deena waved over her shoulder. She was on it.

"Hey, boss," said Mimi, who was wandering

the place dressed as a fairy, on stilts, her tutu torn, her pointed ears covered with rings.

"What's up?"

"I've had a couple of press asking when Sawyer will be here. Shall I give them an ETA, or keep distracting them with the popcorn stand that's not real popcorn?"

"Distract," Petra said with a smile. "They'll figure out soon enough that the art is the star here today."

They both looked across the forecourt right as Daisy, who was chatting with a camera crew about her installation, looked up and gave them a huge smile.

Mimi nodded. "Do you need me for anything else?"

"No, just carry on doing what you're doing," Petra said.

Mimi grinned, checked her earpiece, then stalked off to make sure everything ran smooth as silk.

Leaving Petra to sigh gustily. Her head was fuzzy, as if she was listening to the conversations around her while her head was underwater. Because, wonderful as the event was, she wished Sawyer was there to see it. Not for the press. Or good PR. But because he'd been a part of this too.

Just because she'd been brave, and strong, in saying *no* to having her heart completely smashed, didn't mean she could just switch it off. Forget all of the lovely moments they'd experienced together over the past weeks.

It didn't mean she could just fall out of love.

Maybe that was her true curse. Doomed to love him for the rest of time.

Sighing again, Petra stared up at the façade of the gallery, which a week before had been dirty old brick in need of a clean. It was now covered in the most beautiful graffiti. Splashes of pink and bronze and white and silver. Beautiful literary quotes, written in chunky block script, each one about the transformative nature of art, the very centre of which sported a sweet daisy tag.

"It's rather a lot, don't you think?"

Petra turned to find her mother standing beside her, looking up at the graffiti art with a discerning eye. "Mum!"

"Darling," Josephine said, leaning in for an air kiss. "Your father is off somewhere bobbing for candy apples. I tried telling him the last thing his heart needs at his age is that much sugar, but alas, he stopped listening to me some time ago."

"You're here," Petra said, her sloshy brain taking a while to catch up with her eyes.

"Of course I'm here. I am on the board."

Josephine's gaze swept over Petra's pink tulle dress, her aubergine lucky boots and the cropped quilted yellow jacket she'd chosen in the hope it might make her look vibrant and happy, even if she wasn't feeling it.

Her gaze was long-suffering, and yet impressed at the same time, as she met Petra's eyes and said, "Also, my daughter is the curator of this outstanding event."

Petra swallowed. Smiled. Then drew her mother in for a quick hug. "Thank you. Now, shall I introduce you to any of the young artists…help you find something new to put up at the house?" she said, so glad to have something to take her mind off the heaviness in her head.

"Oh, I don't know," said Josephine. "There was a rather dapper-looking clown bust back there. Could pop it in my office, to test the state of my patients' hearts."

Petra sniffed out a laugh, which was about as much as she could muster.

Her mother, an efficient woman who'd done what she'd gone there to do, made to move off, only she stopped and said, "I was hoping you might come over for dinner, you and Sawyer. Some time next week."

Petra held her breath, waiting for the disclaimer. When that seemed to be the extent of her mother's offer, she said, "I'd love to." And meant it. "But it would only be me."

Her mother looked harder. Saw enough to understand.

Petra swallowed. "Would this be for Finn's birthday, Mum?"

"Yes, it would." Then, "I spoke to Sawyer on

the phone the other day—did he tell you? No, I can see by your expression he did not. He'd been away and came home to find you not there. He was worried about you. In fact, the dinner was his idea."

Petra shook her head. *What the—? What?*

"He was a big bear of a boy," her mother said. "Only he had the gentlest heart. Much more your kind of person than Finn's. Even then." Another air-kiss. "You've done a wonderful thing here today, darling. You should feel immensely proud of yourself."

Then she was gone. Leaving Petra feeling utterly befuddled.

Sawyer. Calling her mother. Helping her open up about Finn. And taking no credit. Just helping, behind the scenes. Not for the glory, but because it was a kind thing to do.

Sawyer. *Her kind of person...*

She'd pushed Sawyer away, believing that, deep down, he'd not changed. When the truth was he *hadn't* changed. He was the same strong, determined, protective man he'd always been. A man who thought of everyone important in his life before he'd ever consider himself.

If he'd made plans to leave, it wasn't due to a fear of intimacy, or because she was not enough for him; the past weeks *had* proven that. It was because, for some stupid reason, he'd convinced himself that would be best for *her*.

While she, for some other stupid reason, had

never told him that *he* was what was best for her. And always had been.

Only now...now it really was too late. Wasn't it?

The event was going brilliantly. She'd done her part, meaning if she wanted to duck away, she most certainly could. She checked her watch, only to find she'd left Do Not Disturb on. Again.

Turning it off, she saw several notifications come flying up on the screen.

The only one that registered was from Sawyer: nothing but an address.

Petra looked from the pin on the map app on her phone to find herself facing a three-storey building, the exterior a stark matte black, even the windows were blacked out.

Only the golden cage-shaped doorknobs on the big shiny double black doors were indicative of what was inside.

Sawyer had asked her to meet him at the Gilded Cage.

Was this some full circle moment? Had she left something in Lost Property? Was he returning to the scene of the crime to say goodbye for ever? Did it matter?

This was her chance to put the record straight. To tell him how she truly felt. To let him know that her heart was his to do with as he pleased, whether he wanted it or not.

She gave the handle a tug, not surprised to find it opened at her touch.

And inside—it looked so different in the daylight. Empty. And gargantuan. Devoid of all the bodies and the loud music, she could really take in the amazing patterns in the floor, the textures in the soft furnishings, the detail in the twirling gilt around the private booths.

Petra didn't spot Sawyer till she reached the bottom of the stairs leading to the dance floor.

He was at the bar. Battered leather jacket on his back, dark curls catching the light from the disco ball above. Standing in the same spot as that first night.

He turned when her boot heels clacked against the dance floor. And her heart, her poor squidgy besotted heart, flipped over in her chest at the sight of him. At the look in his eyes.

For he looked determined. A man on a mission. Not the kind of mission that had sent him off to far-flung lands again and again. The kind that had taken her by the hand and led her to his bed.

She could only hope with all her might that for once their missions did not clash. Or sending them spinning apart. Maybe this time they might finally be in sync.

Nerves zinging, hope riding a roller coaster, Petra lifted her chin, walked across the dancefloor, dumped her handbag on a pink leather stool and looked along the bar.

"Hey," said Sawyer, his voice rough. His eyes were dark and deep, as if he'd slept about as well as she had.

"Hey," she said back.

"So, I heard from Daisy that there's this amazing festival happening down at the Gallery of Melbourne this weekend."

Petra's lungs squeezed as she laughed out a breath. "Heard the same thing."

He smiled. "It's going well?"

"Beyond well," she said.

Then Sawyer breathed deep and slow, his gaze taking her in. Eating her up, as if he'd been starved of her. Till his gaze landed on her collarbone. On the thin rose gold chain, and the pull tab dangling thereon. The necklace she'd not taken off. Even after telling him it was over. Even after walking away.

When his eyes lifted back to hers they were molten. Focused. Ready. "So, I have a question for you."

She swallowed. "Okay."

"New York, or Germany?"

Not the question she'd been expecting. "Sorry?"

"You mentioned, as you twirled in the rain that night, that you'd fielded offers from a gallery in New York and an underground movement of some kind that made no sense to me in Germany. Have you decided which you'll take on?"

She *knew* it. He'd believed she was leavi

him. Her chest rose and fell as she said, "I field offers all the time, Sawyer. I'm rather a big name in my world. But I'd not made any plans to take up either. Not without talking to you first."

He took the hit. As if he'd figured it out belatedly too.

Then he said, "After I take this final trip for Big Think, I was thinking I'd like to stay on here. For a bit."

"Final trip?" she asked, only able to focus on one bombshell at a time.

He nodded. "I'm heading all over, South and Central America, North Africa, South Asia, to introduce my contacts overseas to their new Big Think team. After which they'll do the heavy lifting, for I'll officially no longer be the brawn of the operation."

Petra breathed deep. "Wow. That's huge, Sawyer." And maybe even partly her doing, pushing as she had for him to imagine what *his* dreams might be. "If you're not going to be that, what *will* you be?"

"Whatever I want," he said. Then he pushed away from the bar and strolled towards her, till he was right there. Right in front of her. All big strong shoulders and warm skin and those clear blue eyes. "Wherever I want."

"And where's that?" she asked, her voice now a whisper.

"I'm thinking I might buy a place. A home, in

fact. One I was hoping you'd like to come back to too."

"Sawyer," she said, feeling woozy and wonderful.

He leant against the bar, his gaze roving over her face. "I should have told you all this last night."

"Hell, yes, you should! Why didn't you?"

"According to Hadley, I was an idiot, and I think she was right."

Petra shook her head. "No, you're not. You're considered. And considerate. And you never say things you don't mean. Which means if you're here now, saying these things to me—" She couldn't finish her thought. It was too big to hold onto.

"I have good reason." Then he smiled. Not *the* smile, the one that blinded and distracted and could take out a pair of knees at fifty paces. But the one he seemed to save for only her

Breathing deep, he lifted a hand and it into her hair, cradling her face. His th her cheek before his eyes once ag

"I love you, Petra."

The sound that spille half laugh, half sob, p it for so long, only it.

"I've pined of the worl ing into

I loved you despite all the reasons I should not. I don't want to do that any more. I want to…go on adventures, and eat too much, find some fabulous little place with a view and spend the day in bed with you."

His words felt so familiar. Then she remembered—the sweetener she'd used to try to get him to promise to marry her. Because she'd loved him for that long too.

At which point she threw herself into Sawyer's arms with enough gusto he rocked back a step. And another. His arms wrapping around her to catch her, to hold her. To pull her close.

"I love you," she said. "I've always loved you. And I want the adventures and the food and the bed. And the place to come home to. All of it, so long as you're there."

He pulled her closer, murmuring, "And if that isn't just the best news I've had all day…"

"Me too," she said, snuggling closer. Absorbing how real he felt. Not fake, not pretend, but honest and true.

Sawyer pulled back. "One more thing?"

"Sure!" She laughed. "But it's been a hell of a day, and I'm not sure I can take much more."

Smiling at her, all blue-eyed and stubbled and big and he said, "The last time we were here I made a hash of something. Something I tried, I made a hash of didn't take."

Sawyer slipped away from her then, and slowly dropped to one knee. "I'm hoping third time's the charm."

"Sawyer," she whispered.

Only this time she didn't freak out. Or beg for him to get the hell up. This time she leaned in—to her racing heart and her wild thoughts, and all the feelings filling her up inside.

"Petra Gilpin, you are my best friend. My muse. The reason I've been able to look at my life and make choices that have me feeling excited about the rest of my life. Marry me. Be with me. Put up with me. Travel with me. Tell me when I'm being an ass. Forgive me." He took in a deep breath. "And love me."

Petra took a moment, soaking in every slash of light, every flutter of dust, every glint of colour, imprinting it on her mind's eye. The moment, the most beautiful work of art she'd ever experienced.

"Petra?" Sawyer warned, his voice rough, impatient.

And her focus contracted to find him holding a ring box. Not pretend. Not a place holder. A pink diamond surrounded by petals of white diamonds, on a rose gold band. Turned out Petra was a ring girl after all.

"Yes!" she blurted. "Yes, a thousand times yes."

Sawyer slipped the ring onto her finger, a perfect fit. Then he winced as he pulled himself to standing.

"Your leg!" Petra said, helping to haul him up. Only to squeak when he grabbed her, twirled her, dipped her and kissed her soundly.

He only broke the kiss to release her laughter, the sound seeming to float up to the ceiling and bounce off the chandelier above.

"So what now?" she asked, tugging on his shirt, tidying it up. Then making it messy again, evidence of their kiss fine with her. "I'm jobless and you're homeless…"

"How do you feel about sleeping in tents and tree houses and tiny backwater hotels with me for a while?"

"I can come? I can come!" Petra had never been to so many of the places Sawyer intended to go. The things she'd see, the culture, the beauty, the art. "How much luggage am I allowed? I have lucky outfits to consider. And then there's Russell—"

Sawyer coughed out a laugh. "Now, hang on a second—"

"He'd not understand if I leave him behind."

Sawyer swore beneath his breath, but his eyes grew dark. "Fine, Russell can come. And can I just say how glad I am to have got to know you all over again, as a grown-up?"

"You may," she said, sliding her hand lower, over his backside. Lifting her leg to tuck it around his calf.

Then they kissed for a very long time. By the

time they came up for air Sawyer's curls were mussed, and Petra's clothes didn't look much better.

"Shall we get out of here?" Sawyer asked.

Petra wrapped her arm through his, her head tucked into his shoulder as they made their way across the dance floor. Under the light of the disco ball Sawyer twirled her out to the end of his arm and back again. Only this time she stuck. For good.

Mimi took over Petra's fundraising job at the gallery and did a far better job of that than Petra ever could.

After Finn's birthday dinner at the Gilpin family home, a reserved affair till her mum got into the port, after which things took a quite nice turn, Petra and Sawyer, and a Big Think contingent, set off.

For the next few weeks they travelled everywhere together, before Petra split off to New York for a spell. Back and forth they went, making sure to all be home for the Big Think Ball. Sawyer full to the brim with ideas on how to get the The Big Think Centres for Physical Therapy project underway, and plans to spend time with his family because he wanted to, not because he felt he should.

The first chance they had – between Petra decking out chalets and recording studios and her parents' home with the most wondrous arrays of art—they settled on a beautiful, new, gloriously eclectic hideaway in the Dandenong mountains, where they watched movies on the couch, kept bowls filled with found things on every surface and lived such normal lives, while clearly ridiculously in love.

And those who noticed barely batted an eyelid.

* * * * *

Look out for the next story in the Billion-Dollar Bachelors trilogy

Cinderella Assistant to Boss's Bride

coming soon!

And, if you enjoyed this story, check out these other great reads from Ally Blake

Whirlwind Fling to Baby Bombshell
The Wedding Favor
The Millionaire's Melbourne Proposal

Available now!